## ALSO BY ALLISON VARNES

*Property of the Rebel Librarian*

# Say it out Loud

## ALLISON VARNES

RANDOM HOUSE NEW YORK

Text copyright © 2021 by Allison Varnes
Jacket art copyright © 2021 by Julie McLaughlin

All rights reserved. Published in the United States by Random House Children's Books, a division of Penguin Random House LLC, New York.

Random House and the colophon are registered trademarks of Penguin Random House LLC.

Visit us on the Web! rhcbooks.com

Educators and librarians, for a variety of teaching tools, visit us at RHTeachersLibrarians.com

*Library of Congress Cataloging-in-Publication Data*
Name: Varnes, Allison, author.
Title: Say it out loud / Allison Varnes.
Description: First edition. | New York : Random House, [2021] | Audience: Ages 8–12. | Summary: Self-conscious of her stutter, Charlotte says nothing as her best friend is bullied, but as the school year goes on she realizes some things are worth speaking up for.
Identifiers: LCCN 2020025691 (print) | LCCN 2020025692 (ebook) | ISBN 978-1-5247-7151-5 (trade) | ISBN 978-1-5247-7152-2 (lib. bdg.) | ISBN 978-1-5247-7153-9 (ebook)
Subjects: CYAC: Stuttering—Fiction. | Bullying—Fiction. | Friendship—Fiction. | Middle schools—Fiction. | Schools—Fiction.
Classification: LCC PZ7.1.V398 Say 2021 (print) | LCC PZ7.1.V398 (ebook) | DDC [Fic]—dc23

Printed in the United States of America
10  9  8  7  6  5  4  3  2  1
First Edition

For the girl on the bus

# CONTENTS

CHAPTER 1: Two Truths and a Lie. . . . . . . . . . . . . . . . . . . . . . . . . . . . . 1

CHAPTER 2: Domino Effect . . . . . . . . . . . . . . . . . . . . . . . . . . . . . . 4

CHAPTER 3: This Isn't Kansas . . . . . . . . . . . . . . . . . . . . . . . . . . . . . 16

CHAPTER 4: C-c-cry . . . . . . . . . . . . . . . . . . . . . . . . . . . . . . . . . . . 25

CHAPTER 5: The Bad Thing. . . . . . . . . . . . . . . . . . . . . . . . . . . . . . 38

CHAPTER 6: After the Fall . . . . . . . . . . . . . . . . . . . . . . . . . . . . . . 42

CHAPTER 7: One Day Late . . . . . . . . . . . . . . . . . . . . . . . . . . . . . . 50

CHAPTER 8: The Biggest Chicken at Carol Burnett Middle . . . . . 58

CHAPTER 9: Auditions . . . . . . . . . . . . . . . . . . . . . . . . . . . . . . . . . 65

CHAPTER 10: Secret Friends . . . . . . . . . . . . . . . . . . . . . . . . . . . . . 81

CHAPTER 11: The Beginning of the End . . . . . . . . . . . . . . . . . . . . . 96

CHAPTER 12: It's Not Fair . . . . . . . . . . . . . . . . . . . . . . . . . . . . . . 103

CHAPTER 13: The First Sparks . . . . . . . . . . . . . . . . . . . . . . . . . . . 112

CHAPTER 14: Something Wicked . . . . . . . . . . . . . . . . . . . . . . . . . . 126

CHAPTER 15: Timing . . . . . . . . . . . . . . . . . . . . . . . . . . . . . . . . . . 143

CHAPTER 16: Staging. . . . . . . . . . . . . . . . . . . . . . . . . . . . . . . . . . 150

CHAPTER 17: Fame . . . . . . . . . . . . . . . . . . . . . . . . . . . . . . . . . . . 154

CHAPTER 18: I'm a WHAT?. . . . . . . . . . . . . . . . . . . . . . . . . . . . . 168

CHAPTER 19: A Million Letters . . . . . . . . . . . . . . . . . . . . . . . . . . 179

CHAPTER 20: Make Your Mark . . . . . . . . . . . . . . . . . . . . . . . . . . 193

CHAPTER 21: A Shoe-In! . . . . . . . . . . . . . . . . . . . . . . . . . . . . . . . 207

CHAPTER 22: Showtime . . . . . . . . . . . . . . . . . . . . . . . . . . . . . . . 217

CHAPTER 23: It's a Wrap. . . . . . . . . . . . . . . . . . . . . . . . . . . . . . . 228

## CHAPTER ONE

# TWO TRUTHS AND A LIE

"Truth or dare?" Maddie asks from the other couch, her eyes pleading with me to play along.

Like I'd say "dare" again. Last time, I had to give her dog a haircut, and we were both grounded for a month. Her dog didn't seem to mind, though.

"Truth," I say, settling deeper into my sleeping bag on the love seat. We always play Truth or Dare when we have sleepovers, and my parents let us sleep downstairs so we can watch movies later than usual.

"Oh, okay. Fine." Maddie sighs and rolls back onto her pillow. "What scares you more than anything?"

"Clowns," I say immediately.

She giggles. "You're kind of a chicken, Charlotte."

"Am not! You don't like them, either. They're creepy!"

She wiggles her eyebrows at me. "I'm going to make you a stuffed clown for your birthday. At Build-A-Bear."

I shake my head and toss a tiny embroidered pillow at her head. "And it will go straight into the t-trash!" I frown. I hate it when I stutter, even when it's in front of a good friend like Maddie.

Maddie laughs even harder. Her teeth are bright white against her sun-kissed skin. "Aren't you afraid it will climb out and get you?"

"NO!" I shiver at the thought of it. "Okay, your turn. Truth or dare?"

She stops laughing and grows quiet. "Truth."

"What are *you* scared of most?"

Maddie groans. "Really, Charlotte? Can't you think of something else?"

"No. You asked me. Totally fair."

"I don't know. I . . ."

"Come on!" I say. "Out with it!"

"Middle school," she says.

Neither of us laughs this time. After a summer of our usual neighborhood games and sleepovers, middle school starts next week. We haven't talked about it much, but it's still coming. Middle school should've been my answer, too, if I were completely honest.

"What do you think it will be like?" Maddie asks.

"I don't know," I say. I secretly hope it will be like the middle schools I've seen on TV shows, where kids have classes with their friends and they burst into song in the hallway. I know that won't happen, but it's hard to picture a new school. Plus, I've never even ridden the bus! My parents drove me to elementary school every day because they work there. So this year will be completely different. It's going to take a while to get used to it.

"Me neither." She sighs. "I hope we have classes together."

"We will."

Maddie frowns. "It's a big school. What if we don't?"

I prop my head on the back of my arm. Maddie and I have been in the same class since third grade. She's my best friend, and she lives right down the street. I don't want to think about not having a class with her. "What if we d-do?"

## CHAPTER TWO

# DOMINO EFFECT

The gum sinks into Ben Hooper's red hair with a wet *thwack,* and the entire bus falls silent. Well, okay, everyone except for Tristan and Josh, who laugh and high-five each other a few seats back.

Maddie gasps next to me.

I can't believe they actually did it. Tristan and Josh were mean in elementary school, but they're even worse as sixth graders. Middle school might as well be another planet, and it's only week two. Everything is bigger now—the school, the classes, and especially the kids.

But not Ben, who's exactly the same size as he was last year. He reaches behind his pale, freckled neck and pulls the gob forward, stretching long, pink strings across his shoulder. "What is this?" he cries, turning in his seat. The country radio station crackles over the speakers.

I stare at my hands, leaning forward so my long, light brown hair falls around my face and blocks my view. I can't stand to watch.

A voice from the back yells, "What's the matter? You wanted gum!" Several kids laugh.

Ben's lower lip trembles.

I give Maddie a look. We watched him ask almost everyone for gum when he first got on the bus this morning.

The bus driver calls over his shoulder, "Settle down now! No yelling!"

I wish one of the older kids would say something. The bus is full of them, but all they're doing is snickering and filming the drama with their phones. It's going to be all over the school by the end of homeroom.

This is so wrong. But what can I do? They wouldn't listen to me anyway, and if they did—

Maddie pokes my arm. "I'm going to say something," she whispers.

"No," I say. "D-d-don't." I inwardly cringe. Stuttering in public is the worst. My cheeks flood with warmth.

She frowns. "Why not?"

*Because I want to stay invisible, since I'm new to riding the bus. Because if I sit here quietly, there's a chance no one will mess with me and I can escape without gum in my hair.* But I can't say that. I'm already stuttering more because I'm worried, and my speech will just get worse if I try to explain it. Not that Maddie is bothered by that. She's heard me stutter a million times since we met in third grade, and she's never made me feel bad about it. "I don't know. Just stay out of it."

The wheels groan as the bus lurches to a stop. Carol Burnett Middle, here we come.

"It isn't right." Maddie pivots in her seat and eyes Tristan and Josh.

I peek at them over the top of my seat as they gather their things. It's weird how they *look* like nice boys. Josh's fair skin doesn't have a single zit, and his smile is so perfect, he doesn't need braces. Tristan's light brown curls fall perfectly around his tanned face, and he has a small cleft in his chin. Let's face it—they know they're cute, *and* they play football.

"It's not like you can do anything about it," I say, but I might as well be talking to myself. Maddie would fight to the end if she thought she could change something. Last year, she begged her mom nonstop for a cell phone, and it actually worked!

The bus doors open, and Ben disappears down the steps.

Maddie follows me into the aisle. "Who says we can't?"

Oh no. There's no "we" in this. I say nothing as we file off the bus and walk through the back doors of the school. I'm not getting involved. Snack machines line the hallway, and my stomach growls. I wish I'd remembered to grab a granola bar before I left home.

"You don't have an extra dollar, do you?" I ask. I brought only enough money for lunch. Sometimes my dad gives me lunch money for the whole week and throws in extra for snacks, but he didn't today.

"No, sorry."

I sigh. At least I changed the subject. "Oh! I can't believe I almost forgot! Did you ask your mom if you can go see *Wicked* for my birthday?" *The Wizard of Oz* was my favorite movie when I was little, and *Wicked* is about what happened *before* Dorothy went over the rainbow. I've listened to the soundtrack a million times. But it's not enough, because I still don't know the whole story. I *need* to see this show.

Maddie sighs. "I knew I was forgetting something."

"Maddie! Tickets go on sale Friday, and you *know* you love musicals! Write it on your hand."

Maddie nods and twirls her braid like she used to do in math when she was trying to figure out a problem.

The main corridor is packed with groups of kids playing on their phones. Some sit on benches reading books. Others have earbuds in their ears, which is code for *Leave me alone.* I should remember to bring mine for the computer lab. Some seventh-grade girls by the bathroom stop applying lip gloss as we pass. One leans in and whispers to another. I glance down at my jeans and tug at my T-shirt. I don't know why they're staring, but they did it on the first day of school, too. Just past them, Tristan laughs with Josh while he retrieves a few books from his locker. I turn away, but Maddie openly glares at them. We've barely made it to the end of the hallway when the homeroom bell rings, and everyone darts in different directions.

Maddie blurts out, "Tell Mr. Burton that I'll be late," and walks the opposite way.

"Where are you going?" I yell after her.

"There's something I have to do," she calls over her shoulder.

I was afraid of that.

I slump over my novel in English class and read the same paragraph for the third time. I have no idea what it says. I can't think. I can't focus on anything because Maddie never made it to homeroom. What could possibly be taking so long? All she had to do was walk to the office, tell them what happened, and come straight back. No big deal.

But *of course* it's a huge deal. If Tristan or Josh finds out what she did, everything will change, and—

The phone rings.

Ms. Harper puts down her book and answers the classroom phone on the second ring. "This is Ms. Harper, educating young minds and making the world a better place. How may I help you?" She tucks a stray strand of light brown hair behind her ear.

I grin into my hand. I love it when she answers the phone. She teaches English and musical theater, and I have her for both.

She turns and fixes her gaze on me. "Sure, I'll send her." With a click, she hangs up and then says, "Charlotte, they need you in the office."

The smile drains from my face. I didn't do anything. My heart pounds. I reach for my bag and feel everyone's eyes following me as I walk to the door. Getting called out in front of the whole class is the worst. I hate that this is happening when *I told Maddie* that I didn't want to be involved. I didn't see anything, and even if I did, no good ever comes from being a snitch. Everyone knows that.

I drag myself down the endless hallway, glancing up at the bulletin boards as I go. I'd already be at the office by now if I were in my old elementary school, but Carol Burnett Middle is five times as big, with five times as much wall art. There are inspirational quotes painted in different colors on the walls near the office. BE THE DIFFERENCE, THE CHOICE

IS YOURS, blah, blah, blah. It's a bunch of encouraging stuff from famous dead people. I wish they had some advice for what to do when you see a kid get pelted with gum.

I take a deep breath and pull the door open, the bell at the top jingling against the glass. The entire front office is full of kids from my bus. This can't be happening. I don't even know what *this* is, but it can't be good. I tug at my collar, which all of a sudden feels like it's choking me. I walk up to the receptionist, who has a fire engine–red pixie cut.

"Name?" she says, peering at me from behind pink-rimmed glasses.

"Charlotte Andrews," I say.

A deep voice from the hallway booms, "Have a good day." The secretary glances over her shoulder as Maddie walks toward us.

I open my mouth, but the words don't come.

Maddie's wide eyes meet mine. A flicker of guilt crosses her face, and then something stronger replaces it. She holds her chin a little higher.

"Take a seat," the secretary says, crossing my name off a list on her desk. Her nails have tiny flames painted on them. "No talking."

Maddie's brown eyes plead with me as she passes by. It's like she's saying, *Do the right thing, Charlotte.* Why does doing the right thing have to involve the principal's office?

I perch on the edge of the stained fabric chair. One of the older kids from the bus stares at me.

The receptionist answers the office phone. "Will do!" she says. Turning to me with a sigh, she says, "Mr. Sinclair will see you now, Charlotte." I almost trip over my shoe, but I catch myself just in time.

I walk as quickly as I can to the open office door. Mr. Sinclair sits behind his huge desk in a navy pin-striped suit, the deep bronze of his scalp shiny under the humming fluorescent lights.

"Ms. Andrews! Thank you for coming."

Like I had a choice. If it were up to me, I'd still be reading my book in English.

"We need to discuss an incident that happened on your bus this morning."

"Okay." I squirm in my seat.

He holds up a cell phone displaying a picture of Ben pulling strings of gum out of his hair. Wow. That really did travel fast. "Do you know anything about this?"

*Don't fidget. Just stay calm. It's all going to be okay.* "Ben g-got gum in his hair."

Mr. Sinclair's expression softens, probably because I stuttered. I hate the moment when someone realizes I'm different. It changes the way they look at me. "And how did that happen?"

"Someone threw it."

"And how do you know they threw it?"

I gulp. "Just g-guessing."

"Mmm. Did you see who threw that gum?"

"No." Which is true—I really didn't.

He leans back in his leather chair. "How far away from Ben were you sitting?"

I shrug and look down at my hands. "I don't know. He was on the right near the front. I was a few seats b-back on the left."

"I see. So you were maybe, what, eight feet away?"

"I guess."

Mr. Sinclair makes a note on a piece of paper on his desk. "Okay, being maybe, oh, eight feet or so away, you didn't see *anything*?" He tilts his head, his eyebrows knitted together.

"No." My voice travels up too high.

He sighs. "That's too bad, Ms. Andrews. I was hoping you'd be able to help us find out who did this to Ben. We've interviewed some students and the bus driver, and we still don't have the answers." He puts down his pen. "Bullying is not tolerated at this school."

"N-no, sir."

He studies me for a minute. I look away while my face warms. I always stutter worse when I'm nervous or excited, which has been every minute of middle school so far.

"Do you have any idea who might have thrown the gum?"

Oh no. He changed the question, and now I can actually say something. I know it had to be Tristan and Josh. I can still hear them laughing. But I didn't *see* them do it. I shrug.

"Okay." He hands me a clipboard. "I'd like you to write a brief statement, then. In your own words, tell me what happened."

I sigh and pick up a pencil. I scribble out, Someone threw gum into Ben Hooper's hair on the bus this morning. I didn't see who did it. I pause with my pencil still to the paper. That's all I'm going to write. I'm safe with that. But with a twinge of guilt, I realize that Ben won't be.

Mr. Sinclair says, "And whatever you write is strictly confidential."

I look up at him. He didn't say that before. What am I supposed to do? If I tell, it could come back to me, but if I don't . . . Tristan and Josh will get away with it. I can't let that happen. It could've been me instead of Ben. It could've been any of us. "P-promise?" I look away from him when I start to stutter.

"No student will know you wrote it."

*Do the right thing, Charlotte.* Maybe this will stop them. But if Mr. Sinclair doesn't keep his word, if anyone finds out . . . I don't even want to think about it. I wipe my sweaty hand on my jeans. I know what I should do, but actually *doing* it is much harder. It's a million times easier than saying it, though. Writing it means there are no words to stumble over or embarrassing stares when I mess up. I take a deep breath. I have to do this for Ben. My hand shakes as I write, *But I heard them laughing. It was Tristan and Josh.*

Somehow I manage to put the words on paper. I may have been silent on the bus, but at least I'm telling the truth now. No one deserves what they did to Ben. And as I sign my name to the bottom of the page, I feel so much better.

Mr. Sinclair beams at me. "Thank you for your help, Ms. Andrews. Let's hope we won't have to call on you again."

As I walk out of his office, I notice another room with a big table. And sitting at that table is Ben, his eyes swollen, and a woman with red hair patting his shoulder. It must be his mom. She looks up, and I quickly move away from the doorway. Part of me wants to say something to try to make it better, but I can't find the words. I fix my eyes on the exit sign and walk quickly down the hallway.

In the waiting area, Tristan and Josh sit huddled together. Tristan glances up at me, then whispers something to Josh. They both stare as the secretary signs my note so that I can return to class.

My empty stomach gurgles. Stay calm. It's okay. I just wrote what I thought happened. And *signed my name* to it. I was in there a while, too. What was I thinking? That I was going to be a secret snitch and ride off into the sunset? Maybe if I could ride a horse, but too bad for me, I'm riding the bus.

The bell jingles as the office door shuts behind me, and my heart flip-flops.

When they get in trouble, they're going to know someone told. Someone like me. Like Maddie. And even if they never find out who did it, it won't matter. They'll decide who's guilty.

I think they already did.

## CHAPTER THREE

# THIS ISN'T KANSAS

I still haven't gotten used to middle school lunch. In elementary school, the cafeteria was okay because I knew everyone. But now, all the kids from three elementary schools are in one middle school. And it feels like I don't know anyone at all, and the ones I do know don't want to know me or have different lunch periods. Maybe I can just sit on a bench and eat in the lobby. Anything would be better than this.

At the door, the teacher on lunch duty jumps up and blocks my path. "Where are you going?"

"The lobby."

"Not with that tray. Food stays in the cafeteria."

This is one of the worst days ever. There's no escape.

I scan the tables and zero in on one near the back with some empty seats. No one even looks up when I sit down. I'm completely invisible. I poke at the soggy carrots with my spork. If only Maddie had the same lunch period. We sat together every day in fifth grade, and now . . . I don't know what to do. I have no one. I didn't think it was possible to be surrounded by people all the time and feel so lonely.

After lunch, it's social studies, and then PE.

Finally I go to musical theater, which I'm taking only because my mom made me. I begged and pleaded all summer to get out of it, but she wouldn't budge. She said, "But, sweetie, you *love* musicals!"

I said, "That doesn't mean I want to be in one!"

She gave me a look—the one that says, *Of course you do.*

"Mom . . . I'm going to stutter in front of everyone. I can't do it!"

Mom said, "Charlotte, we've been over this. You don't stutter when you sing, and you have such a great voice! It might even help you get more comfortable standing up and speaking in front of people." Before I could say another word, she added, "And it's high time you got involved in a group. You might make some really good friends. Do this for a year, and if you hate it, you can quit."

"But what if I embarrass myself in front of everyone?" As far as I was concerned, there was no other way for it to go.

Mom hooked her arm around my shoulders and squeezed. "What if you love it?"

I glared up at her.

"Just sing, Charlotte. It's going to be okay," she said, dropping a kiss onto my forehead before I could duck out of the way.

It's been fine so far. I sing, and no one really notices me . . . except Ms. Harper. She smiles at me after each song. Is she just being nice? Does she like my voice? Or has she seen that official piece of paper explaining that I go to speech? If she has, it's just a matter of time before she pulls me aside to talk about it and I'll want to crawl under a desk and hide.

Right before Ms. Harper and Ms. Bishop, the chorus teacher, bring musical theater class to an end, Ms. Harper says, "I know you've all been waiting to hear which musical we'll be performing—"

"Can we do *Hamilton*?" blurts out Jack, his black hair swooping down over his deep brown eyes and olive complexion. He's in sixth grade, same as me. I smile. He'd be such a good Alexander Hamilton! But then I realize I'm flashing my braces at the world, so I quickly cover my teeth.

"No, let's do *Legally Blonde*," says Aubrey, flipping her

long blond hair over her perfectly tanned shoulder. "I'd be the best Elle! I have stage *and* screen experience!"

I sigh. She's been in community children's show choir since first grade. Then she did a local commercial for a car dealership over the summer, where she climbs into a car and says, "Gee, Dad, look at all the legroom!" It's the goofiest thing ever. If it were me, I'd never be able to live it down. But it just made her a more popular seventh grader, and people are even saying she's going to get a free car when she turns sixteen. Part of me wants to say, *The commercial isn't that great.* It wouldn't matter, though. Everyone treats her like she's the star of a new TV show.

Ms. Harper frowns and says, "I'll wait for you."

When no one else speaks, she says, "We're going to perform *The Wizard of Oz.*"

I gasp. Is this for real? I know the words to *every* song. I could sing it in my sleep, I know it so well! Maybe this means I won't embarrass myself. Maybe this means I could actually *like* this class.

"Auditions will be during class next Monday in the auditorium."

My jaw drops. Monday? That's not enough time! But at least I know all the words. If I practice all weekend, it will be okay. Maybe.

Ms. Harper continues. "You should prepare sixteen bars

of a song from any musical *except* this one and bring the sheet music. You'll be expected to read lines for the character you want to audition for, and then we'll do a dance tryout. Sound good?"

NO! I know other musicals, sure, but not like *The Wizard of Oz.* I can't read lines without messing up. And what was that she said about dancing? So much for not embarrassing myself. This is going to be a disaster.

"Oh, and please don't make us listen to 'On My Own' again," she adds. "I can't take it anymore after last year."

Ms. Bishop chuckles and pushes her glasses higher on her freckled nose.

Well, there goes *Les Misérables.*

The bell rings.

"Have a good afternoon!" says Ms. Harper, her blue eyes sparkling against her tan. "Make good choices! Think about audition songs!"

I fight the sea of kids to get to my bus, and slide into a seat. My mind is racing with ideas for the audition. I could sing one of Audrey's songs from *Little Shop of Horrors*! I've always liked that show. Or maybe something from *Beauty and the Beast.* I could totally sound like Belle.

The doors shut, and the engine whines as the bus pulls away from the curb. I prop myself on my elbows and look around the half-full bus. That's weird. I knew Ben wouldn't be here, but neither is Maddie. I swallow the lump forming in my throat as I realize that Tristan and Josh are also missing.

Maybe they just checked out early. Their parents could've picked them up for an appointment or something. Or they could be staying late for an after-school activity. But I know that's not what happened.

I let myself in through the front door, spread peanut butter onto a graham cracker, and go upstairs to my room. My parents won't be home for another hour or so, since they're still at the elementary school. Dad is a school counselor, and Mom teaches fourth grade. I miss the time when we all went to school together and I didn't have to ride the bus to Carol Burnett Middle.

I pick up the phone to call Maddie, but I put it down mid-dial. I don't even know what to say to her right now. She knew I wanted to stay out of it, and yet she gave them my name. At least, I think she did. Maybe I'm wrong and they were going to interview the whole bus anyway. I don't know.

I try to work on my homework, but all I can think about is Maddie. Where did she go? Is she okay? I finally close my books and wander downstairs to distract myself. When my parents walk through the door, they find me streaming *The Wizard of Oz*. It's the part where Glinda asks the Wicked

Witch of the West if she's forgotten about the slippers. Glinda has a huge smile on her face.

Mom clears her throat. "What about your homework?" She's a lot taller than I am, which means maybe I might actually grow this year. We have the same light brown hair, and even our complexions are alike: fair skin that flushes bright pink every time we get embarrassed. I pause the movie. "It *is* homework."

Dad laughs, the lines around his blue eyes crinkling behind his glasses. His eyes are the same color as mine. Unfortunately, I also got my vision from him. My parents made me start wearing glasses last year when I couldn't see the whiteboard at school. "Uh-huh. Books first. You can watch TV when you finish." He heads for the kitchen.

"But we're going to perform *The Wizard of Oz* in musical theater!"

Mom crashes onto the couch next to me. "Ah, your favorite! That's wonderful, sweetie." She grins. "Being in a musical might not be so bad after all, huh? I think you're going to like it!"

"Maybe," I say. It's one thing to watch *The Wizard of Oz*, but it's totally different to perform it. I just don't know if I can do it. I frown. I *definitely* can't dance.

"When are auditions?" Mom asks.

"Next week. I think I might sing a song from *Beauty and the Beast*."

She nods. "You'd feel okay with that one?"

"Maybe," I say, but only because I know I won't stutter during the song. It's the only time I can be like everybody else. If the world could sing all the time instead of speak, my life would be so different.

"*Maybe?* You'll totally knock it out of the park!"

I shrug. "I'm just so nervous." The thought of singing alone, with everyone staring at me, makes my heart beat faster. What if I mess up?

"Just *sing*, Charlotte. Who wouldn't love that gorgeous voice of yours?" she says with a smile. "Which character are you going to try out for?"

"I haven't decided yet."

"You can't go wrong. Just don't forget about your other homework."

"I won't! P-promise."

"Oh, and I'm going to let you set the table."

I grin. "You're going to *let* me?"

"Yup. It's all yours." She pries herself off the couch and joins Dad in the kitchen to make dinner. After a minute, it sounds like they're starting a rock band with pots and pans.

I reach for the remote and glance up at Glinda's face on the screen. I don't know why I never noticed it before, but she looks happy to have just asked the witch about the slippers. *Too* happy. I know what happens next: the Wicked

Witch reaches for the slippers, but before she can touch them, they vanish and reappear on Dorothy's feet. I frown. I always thought Glinda was this kind lady who helped Dorothy. But with that smile, she looks a lot like Tristan and Josh did when the gum landed in Ben's hair.

## CHAPTER FOUR

# C-C-CRY

The next morning, I slide into the bus seat next to Maddie. "Hey."

"Hey," she says, shutting her red journal. She never lets me see what's in it, but I'll bet I can guess what she just wrote.

I give her an expectant look. *"Well?"*

She sighs. "I'm not supposed to talk about it." A few pieces of her black hair dance in the breeze from the cracked windows.

"You didn't mind talking about it yesterday!"

She glares at me. "I did the right thing, okay? I'm not like you, Charlotte. I can't just pretend it didn't happen."

Maddie has it all wrong. I start to say that I did the right thing, too, but then Ben boards the bus. He looks around and drops down into the seat closest to the driver. A huge chunk of his hair is missing in the back. Someone cut his hair close to his scalp to remove the gum.

Maddie motions toward the front of the bus and whispers, "And *that's* why I did it."

The bus slowly fills up with more kids as we drive through another section of our neighborhood. It's like the cafeteria all over again. Most of them are older than me, and even though I remember their faces from elementary school, I don't know all their names. They play on their cell phones, listen to music, or sprawl across their seats talking to friends until they have to make room for someone else. My ears perk up at a Dolly Parton song playing on the radio, but this is no time for singing. Tristan appears first on the landing, then Josh. They grin when they spot Ben, but they keep walking toward their usual spot closer to the back of the bus.

"Just so you know," I say, "I think—" Tristan and Josh fall into the seat behind us. I freeze, my words forgotten. My heart dances a frantic rhythm fueled by cold adrenaline. Each second feels like an eternity.

Maddie takes a deep breath and stares straight ahead.

Tristan hooks his elbows over the seat and says, "Hey, Josh! I think we found the snitch!"

I want to cry. I knew they'd figure it out. They're going to make us pay for this.

His voice is smooth and soft. "We know it was you. Did you think you were going to get us into trouble?" He laughs. "Aww, you did! That's hilarious."

Josh pops up over the back of our seat. "We didn't even get detention!"

Seriously? I never would've—

"Except our parents had to meet with the principal all because of your big mouth," Tristan says. "Good thing they couldn't prove anything."

A flicker of anger flashes across Josh's face. "Yeah, that part was messed up. You almost cost us our football game."

Tristan says, "Who *does* that?"

*Stay calm, Charlotte. Breathe.* Maybe if I just don't react, they'll get bored and leave me alone.

Maddie stares straight ahead. She must be thinking the same thing.

"Hey, snitch! I'm talking to you." Tristan kicks the back of Maddie's side of the seat.

She whirls to face them. "You," she says, her voice coming out low and firm, "need to stop. *Now.*"

Both boys laugh.

"Or what?" Tristan smirks. "You'll tell? Yeah, that really worked last time."

She rolls her eyes and turns back around.

Wait, so . . . They're not after *me*? Relief washes over me, and quickly turns to panic.

"You didn't answer my question, loser!" Tristan says. He punches the back of her side of the seat a lot harder this time and laughs.

Maddie clenches her jaw.

If only someone would help. I glance at the kids watching in the seats around us, but they look away. I can't just sit here. My heart hammers in my chest and drowns out their laughter. I have to *do* something. "Stop!" I say, the word falling out of my mouth before I can talk myself out of it.

"Oh, look, another one! They come in pairs. Hey, UGLY!" Josh strikes the back of my seat so hard, it feels like he's punching me right between my shoulder blades. I gasp. I know I'm ugly, but I wasn't prepared for someone to actually say it. He has no idea that he doesn't need to hit my seat. The word hurts more.

"Cut it out!" Maddie says.

"Make me!" *Punch.* "Rejects!" *Punch.* They beat the backs of our seats together in a perfect left-right, left-right rhythm that blends with the humming engine and the radio. We lean away from the back of the seat to escape the continuing blows. Our eyes meet. Maddie shakes her head.

"Hey!" *Punch!*

"D-don't!" I yell, and immediately cringe. I know better than to start with a hard sound like *D*, but I didn't even think about it. It just came out.

"D-d-d-don't!" Tristan mimics. "Talk much?" He laughs.

My heart races off to break somewhere far away from here, leaving me reeling. The warmth rises up my face until it reaches my eyes, and then they're leaking and there's nothing I can do about it.

"Hello, I asked you a qu-qu-qu-question—" *Punch.*

I choke back a sob. I've been so careful not to let anyone hear me stutter. I don't get loud, I try to speak slowly, and when all that fails, I don't talk unless I really have to. I haven't been in class with those two since second grade, but I guess they forgot. And none of that matters now because I've just announced that I'm different.

Maddie squeezes my arm. "LEAVE. US. ALONE!" she yells.

Josh stops laughing. "Wait! Shh! Shh!" he says, putting his finger to his lips. "Listen!" After a second he says, "That's weird. I thought I heard something just now. Did you hear it?"

"Nope," Tristan says with a shrug. "Didn't hear a thing."

The loudspeaker crackles. "You all need to settle down, or every person on this bus is going straight to the principal's office," the bus driver says. "I mean it!"

That doesn't sound like a bad idea, all things considered. *Punch.*

The gears groan as the bus chugs up the drive to the drop-off area, and we roll to a halt. *Stop crying, you baby. Stop it!* I can't even see because my tears have steamed up my glasses. As I take them off and wipe them on my jeans,

I realize that the punching has finally ended. I put on my glasses and see the boys standing over us, sneering.

Tristan says, "Aw, now I feel bad. Yeah, you're the ugliest girl I've ever seen, but there's no reason to c-c-cry about it."

Josh high-fives him, and they exit the bus.

I breathe in a ragged breath and wipe my nose on my sleeve. I don't even care if it's gross. I'm ugly and everyone knows it, so what does it even matter if I have snot on my shirt?

"You okay?" Maddie asks.

I sniffle. *No. I don't think I'll ever be okay again.* "Yeah, you?"

"Okay."

If only Maddie had just stayed out of it yesterday, things might've worked out. If Josh and Tristan hadn't come after her, if I hadn't tried to help, I wouldn't be feeling like this right now.

Maddie pats my shoulder.

I shrink back from her. I don't know what to say.

The halls are rowdy as usual as we walk to homeroom together. Maddie steals a few glances at me, her eyes full of worry. I walk as close to the wall as I can to force some distance between us. She's practically staring at me when all I want to do is disappear.

"Do you want to talk about it?"

I shake my head and wipe my eyes on my sleeve. I don't ever talk about stuttering with Maddie. I've never had to because she totally ignores it when it happens. There are no questions, no imitations. She listens to *what* I'm saying instead of how I say it. I've never had to explain myself because I think she gets that I would be embarrassed. Why would I want to start explaining now?

Maddie's shoulders fall. "Okay," she says, and darts another concerned glance at me. "I'm sorry, Charlotte." She sets her jaw. "And you are *not* ugly."

We fall silent. We don't talk about musical theater or *Wicked* or doing the right thing. None of it matters. Not really.

"I, uh, gotta go," I say, heading for the bathroom. "See ya in homeroom."

"Charlotte—"

"P-p-please, just go ahead without me."

I dart inside and turn on the faucet at the nearest sink. I splash cold water onto my face and wipe my swollen, red eyes with a paper towel. I don't know why I'm even bothering. It's going to take forever for my face to go back to normal because my eyes are *still* leaking. Great. Way to go, Charlotte. It's just words. Stupid words from stupid boys who don't even know me.

*Then why does it feel like so much more than that?*

I walk into homeroom and take my seat. I try not to look at anyone with my splotchy face, but it's pointless. The guy in front of me turns around and says, "Whoa, who died?"

I think part of me did. I cover my face with my hand and look down.

I broke a major middle school rule. Never let them see you cry.

By the time English begins, I'm an even bigger mess. I want to find a corner and sob, to tell someone what happened. But I can't tell anyone. My heart starts hammering faster. If I squeal, it will just make it worse. I swallow hard. I can't imagine it being worse than this morning. I don't even know if I can ride the bus again. My stomach churns just thinking about it.

Ms. Harper places a note on my desk with my name and a dolphin sticker on it as she passes out papers.

I stare down at the unfamiliar writing. It has to be from a teacher if Ms. Harper gave it to me. My mouth goes dry. I glare at the smiling dolphin sticker, knowing I'm not going to like what's inside. With shaking fingers, I tear open the envelope and read:

> *Hi, Charlotte!*
>
> *I'm your new speech teacher, Ms. Garrett! I'm so excited that we'll be working together this year! I would love to meet you soon. Why don't you swing by*

*my library office during homeroom tomorrow and say
hello? It's going to be a GREAT year!*

*See you soon,*

*Ms. Garrett*

My eyes fill with hot tears. Why can't everyone just leave me alone? I crumple the note into a ball and make it as tiny as I can. My throat tightens. I don't want to be called out of class again—for anything. I can't think about tomorrow right now. Not when I have to survive the bus ride home today. A low gurgling sound rises up from my stomach.

Ms. Harper looks at me funny when she passes by me again. "Are you okay, Charlotte?"

I can't breathe. It's so hot in here.

"Charlotte?" She leans down and speaks in a soft voice, "What's the matter?"

My stomach jerks. Oh no. Not now. I bolt from my seat and race to the door as fast as I can, and right there in front of my entire English class, I vomit a trail of raisin bran.

A few girls scream. One guy yells, "Awesome!"

They all grow quiet, which makes me think Ms. Harper has silenced them with a look.

I get a one-way ticket to the office *again,* and the school nurse calls my mom. I feel so bad that she has to come get me. It's a big deal for her to leave her classroom in the middle of the day because sometimes they can't find a substitute teacher to cover for her. And my dad is always in meetings or helping with testing.

She rushes into the office and puts her hand on my sweaty forehead. "Oh, Charlotte. You're burning up. When did you start feeling sick?"

I tell her the truth. "On the bus."

"Let's get you home. You're not going anywhere today. And maybe not tomorrow, either."

I'm so relieved, I could cry. Again.

We walk out to her beige SUV, which has never looked so beautiful in all my life.

We get in, and she hands me a plastic bag. "Just in case you get sick again."

I nod. "Hey, Mom?"

"Yeah, sweetie?"

"I puked everywhere. Like, in front of everyone. It was so gross. I don't think I can go back." I spewed in front of my favorite teacher, too, and I have her for *two* classes!

Mom starts the engine and backs out of the parking spot. "Did you hit anyone's shoes?"

I half laugh, but it makes my throat hurt, so I stop. "No." At least, I don't think I did. They would have still been screaming if I had. I sigh with relief as the school gets smaller in the mirror outside my window.

"Then it's fine." She gives my shoulder a squeeze. "They'll get over it."

I wish I could say the same.

Being home for two whole days is paradise. Mom fixes me soup with tiny crackers, and we watch musicals together on the couch. So far, we've seen seven. No one punches my seat or makes fun of the way I talk.

On the second day, we're in the middle of watching *Beauty and the Beast* again when the home phone rings.

Mom answers it on the third ring and hands it to me. "Maddie," she whispers.

I pause the movie. "Hello?"

"Hey! Are you feeling better?" Her voice is concerned.

"Uh, I guess," I say.

"When are you coming back?"

"Tomorrow."

Her end of the line goes silent for a moment, and then she says, "Are you okay?"

"I'm not throwing up anymore."

"That's not what I meant, Charlotte. Every time I think about the things Tristan and Josh said, I get so mad!"

My mouth goes dry. I push play to turn the movie back

on and mouth "Sorry" to my mom. Then I disappear up the stairs to my bedroom.

"You're not going to want to do this, but . . ." Maddie takes a deep breath. "I think we should tell."

"No!" I say. "We c-c-can't. That's why we're in this mess."

"But the way they bullied Ben wasn't okay! I'm glad I told. And you know what? The way they're bullying us isn't okay, either!"

My stomach flip-flops, and the nausea creeps back in. I can't handle anything else. I just want it to stop! "Maddie, please. Don't."

"But—"

"I mean it. If you want to tell, fine, but don't b-b-bring me into it, okay?" My heart races.

"Okay, okay!" she says with a huff. Then in a quiet voice, she says, "I won't."

We both fall silent.

This is so weird. We don't fight. Ever. I need to make her understand. "It's just—sometimes telling makes it worse. Like it did for us. What Tristan and Josh are doing now feels even worse."

"Yeah, but . . . sometimes you have to tell. No one can help if they don't know about it." Her mom yells for her in the background. "Hey, I gotta eat dinner." She sighs. "See you tomorrow."

The thought of tomorrow sends a chill across my skin. I reach for a blanket and curl myself into a ball.

Sometimes when a teacher gives a test, and I don't know *anything* on it, I think, *If I just had one more day, I'd be ready!* But this is totally not like that. I could spend all the time in the world at home, and I'd never be ready to ride the bus again.

I want to tell my mom what happened, and that it isn't over. She might understand. But she's my mom, which means it's the law or something that she has to do mom things like tell the principal, and then Tristan and Josh will know *I* told on them. I shudder and snuggle deeper under the blanket.

I can't risk making Tristan and Josh any madder than they already are. They're the problem here. I know that.

So why am I so upset with Maddie?

## CHAPTER FIVE

# THE BAD THING

The next morning I wait for the bus in silence. I'm dreading getting back onto it. But that's not why I'm quiet. It's always quiet at the bus stop. Which is so awkward because my stop is with Lyric, who has refused to act like I exist ever since she started middle school last year. When we were younger, we used to play hide-and-seek and shoot hoops in her driveway until the sun went down. She didn't care that I could never make a basket. And we *always* invited each other to our birthday parties. One year when we were really little, her parents had a petting zoo in their backyard, and we played with the baby goats and ponies for hours. Her mom took a picture of us and put it on their fridge, where it stayed for years. I don't know if it's still there. Once middle school happened, Lyric decided she couldn't talk to me anymore. I thought maybe now that we're both in middle school, we'd be friends again. I was wrong.

The bus pulls up, and the glass doors open with a loud screech. A country song plays on the radio as I start down the aisle. Maddie's seated halfway back on the right, hair in a low ponytail, with a warm smile on her face. As I get closer, she scoots over to the window so I can sit.

I glance at the empty seat next to my best friend, the place where I belong.

And then I keep going.

What did I just *do*? My heart races. Maybe I should go back and sit next to her.

*Do the right thing, Charlotte.*

No, I can't. What would I say? What will she say?

*What will Tristan and Josh do to me today?*

I can't sit with Maddie. And it's too late anyway. I'm already at the back of the bus.

I slide into a seat and crouch down low where Maddie's wounded gaze can't follow. I shut my eyes and lean my forehead against the seat in front of me. The green vinyl smells like sweat and stale gum. I really can't do anything now. You get in big trouble if you leave your seat while the bus is moving.

I sneak a glance to find that Maddie has scooted all the

way to the outer edge of the seat. I couldn't sit with her now even if I wanted to.

The bus moves again, filling up with more kids at each stop, but my heart feels like it's turned to ice.

Finally we arrive at the stop I've been dreading the most.

I duck lower in my seat and wait for the bus to move. I'm taking a big risk, sitting so close to where Tristan and Josh usually sit. But they don't come back this far.

After a minute on the road, I peek over the top of the seat. Tristan is right behind Maddie, leaning over her seat on his elbows, saying who-knows-what to her. Josh is laughing in the seat across from her, his legs spilling out into the aisle. She's all alone because of me. Does the bus driver see what's going on? He doesn't seem to have a clue. Maddie steals a glance back at me so fast, I almost miss her wiping her cheek with her sleeve. I want to run to her seat as fast as I can, but I'm frozen in place. I didn't want to be involved, and now I'm not.

Tristan's arm jerks back like he's about to throw a punch, and then it barrels toward the back of her seat.

I flinch on impact. I can't watch. I steal a glance across the aisle at Lyric, who's also eyeing Maddie's seat. Then she looks directly at me, like she's about to say something, but instead she turns to face the window. I look down at my hands. Does Lyric know I'm supposed to be up there? I swallow the knot forming in my throat and glance back at her. Is this what it feels like to be Lyric? She abandons friends and stays out of things, too. I face the front again. I know what it looks like, but I'm nothing like Lyric. This was just a mistake.

We ride along looking anywhere but there, the sound of cruel laughter swelling with the radio, for the rest of the ride until—

"STOP IT!" Maddie cries.

Even way back here, her voice sounds clear and raw.

The bus lurches to a halt at the drop-off spot, and Maddie pushes her way up the aisle to be one of the first kids off the bus. She doesn't turn around, but she doesn't have to. I can tell she's about to cry again.

How could I do this?

## CHAPTER SIX

# AFTER THE FALL

**E**ach step feels like a million miles on my way to homeroom. I don't want to go. I can't even look at Maddie after what I did, so I completely ignore her when I sit down. While Mr. Burton takes attendance, I sneak a peek out of the corner of my eye. Her eyes are puffy, and her cheeks are splotchy.

It's what I looked like in the mirror on Tuesday, but way worse. At least I wasn't alone when it happened to me.

I'm not supposed to cry anymore when kids laugh and mimic my speech. That was the deal I made with myself this summer. But it feels different on the bus. There are no adults except the bus driver to keep Tristan and Josh from being *really* mean, but he can't see or hear what they're doing. I have no idea if the bus was like this in elementary school, but I definitely don't know how to handle it. And I really don't know what to do about Maddie. I've screwed up, and I'm afraid "sorry" won't be enough to fix it.

Maddie turns and faces me. She lifts her eyebrows as if to say, *Really, Charlotte? I thought you were better than that.* I look down.

The bell rings, and Maddie disappears out the door.

What was I thinking? Oh, right. I *wasn't* thinking. One moment I was walking to our seat, and the next, I acted like I didn't even know her. It only took half a second for me to ruin everything.

I wish she hadn't left so fast. Maybe I could've explained, or tried to, anyway. The shame is killing me. It's all I can do to grab my bag and drag myself to English, where Ms. Harper stands at the open door. "Hey, Charlotte! Hope you're feeling better."

Just when I thought my day couldn't get any worse, I have to face the kids that I puked in front of two days ago. And Ms. Harper. My heart thuds harder. There's no end to the things that I wish I could take back.

"Hi." I force a tight smile and dart into the room, closing the distance between me and my desk in record time. I slide into my seat and wait for the comments. But there's nothing, not even a snicker while I dig in my bag for my notebook and a pencil. When I finally sneak a peek, Ms. Harper is shutting the door behind her, with her gaze fixed on the whole room. Now I get it. They're all behaving because of her. I relax just a bit. Maybe today isn't going to be completely terrible.

We read, we play vocabulary games at the board with a flyswatter, and then Ms. Harper reviews the parts of a story. Just when I find myself believing it's all going to be okay, Ms. Harper says, "Tomorrow we'll discuss a project that we'll work on for the rest of the year."

I inwardly groan. *Please don't say it's a group project.* The thought of giving a presentation makes my stomach queasy all over again.

"You're all going to be writers when you leave this classroom."

I sit up straighter. I wouldn't mind being a writer one day. But does that mean she's going to read my writing? I frown. Maybe that would be okay, as long as I don't have to share with the class. My stomach drops. I won't have to read my stories *out loud*, will I? No matter what I do or where I go, teachers always want me to read out loud, and I hate it. It's like wearing a big sign telling the world that I can't even read a sentence without messing up. I can read. I just can't *say* the words!

The bell rings.

"And that's all for today! More details tomorrow! Make good choices."

I throw my binder into my bag and dart out of the room

with my eyes glued to the floor. Making good choices seems like such a simple thing. If only it were that easy.

The rest of the day passes in a blur. All I can think of is the hurt in Maddie's eyes, and how I'm going to have to see it again soon. It makes my stomach churn, and the sloppy joes they serve at lunch don't help at all.

We play improv games in musical theater, and the next thing I know, the final bell is ringing and it's time to face what I've done.

I feel lost walking through the halls, even though I know exactly where I'm going. After I pass through the double doors and leave school behind me, there's no delaying it. The moment is here. I brace myself and climb aboard the bus. Maddie sits closer to the front this time, shoulders slumped. She looks up at me as I pass. Too late, I notice that she scooted over for me to sit next to her.

It was a chance to make it right, and I missed it! I could turn around right now. Maybe it would be okay. If it wasn't too late a few seconds ago, it's not too late now. No more excuses. I can do this.

I turn back to the front and squeeze past a few kids in the aisle. "Excuse me," I mutter. "Sorry, c-coming through!" Right then, Tristan and Josh reach the top of the bus steps.

I freeze.

"Ugh, sixth graders," an eighth-grade boy grumbles at me. "Move already!"

I stare as Tristan and Josh slide into the seats around Maddie. A huge knot forms in my throat.

"C'mon, move!" another kid says to me.

So I move in the opposite direction, farther away from Maddie, and throw my bag into an empty seat. I hug my knees to my chest and stare out the window as the bus moves away from the curb. I'm the worst friend in the world—if she even considers me a friend anymore.

Later that night, Mom hollers upstairs, "Charlotte! It's time to set the table!"

"Okay!" I'm sprawled across my bed on my stomach, trying to do homework, but I can't really think about anything but Maddie. I close my book and go downstairs.

In the kitchen, Mom removes a pan of rolls from the oven. "What have you been doing up there?"

I make a beeline for the silverware drawer. "Just homework."

She smiles. "Let me know if you need any help."

*I need help. But not with homework.* I shrug. "It's okay. I've got it under control." I stroll over to the cabinet for plates. "Hey, Mom?"

"Mmm?"

"Say you have this friend, um"—my eyes wander to a beach vacation photo on the fridge—"Savannah. And let's say she really hurt another friend's feelings. What could she do to fix it?"

Mom studies me. " 'Sorry' is a good start."

"Yeah, but . . . what if it's too big for 'sorry'?"

"You mean like Savannah needs to *do* something kind?" She makes air quotes with her hands when she says "Savannah," and I cringe.

"Yeah. Like that."

"I still say start with 'sorry.' Say it, mean it, and then never do the hurtful thing again. That's how you fix the situation."

"We're not talking about *me*. We're talking about Savannah."

Mom raises an eyebrow. "Oh, right. That's how *Savannah* should fix it." She adds the final toppings to a tossed salad. "Hey, did Maddie ever give you an answer about *Wicked*? Tickets go on sale tomorrow."

I almost drop my plate. It's not like I can ask Maddie to go with me *now*. What would she say if I had the nerve to call her? Mom may think I can fix it by saying "sorry," but she doesn't know what I—I mean, Savannah—did. I don't think there's a universe where "sorry" is going to work. "She can't make it."

"Oh no! Would it help if I called her mom?" She glances toward the phone on the countertop.

"NO!" My eyes widen. She can't do that! What if her mom knows about the Bad Thing I did? And what if she *tells* my mom?

Mom gives me a sharp look. "Why not?"

"I—I—I mean, no, that's okay," I say, trying to sound super casual. "They, um, have a family thing that night." I force a tight smile. Maybe they do. If they're together in the same room, that's a family thing. I mean, I'm not really lying.

She studies me for a moment. She always knows when something is up. *Keep it together, Charlotte!*

She wipes her hands on a dishtowel and says, "Is there anyone else you'd like to ask?"

My shoulders relax from relief. I shake my head. "Not really." I'd have to actually have friends for that. All the kids that I knew in elementary school have been randomly assigned to different wings in the middle school. I've only seen a few in the hallways here and there.

As if she's heard my thoughts, my mom asks, "Have you gotten to know any of the other kids?"

I shrug. "Haven't really had time yet." *Liar, liar, pants on fire. Again.* I don't know who I am anymore. I *always* tell my mom the truth. It's like one little lie blooms into another one.

She pats my arm. "You will. Wait and see! And we'll have a great time with just the two of us. Are you excited?"

"Yeah!" But as I walk to the table, I feel heavier than I've ever felt before.

## CHAPTER SEVEN

# ONE DAY LATE

It's Friday. Finally. I didn't think this week would *ever* end. All I have to do is make it through today. Just one day. I take a big gulp of chocolate milk. I can do that.

Mom rummages through a cabinet, throwing odds and ends together. She hands me a sack lunch and pats my shoulder. "Today's menu says tuna fish. Thought you'd rather have peanut butter."

I smile up at her. "Thanks." Now that I'm in middle school, I'm supposed to pack my own lunch if I don't want to eat cafeteria food. But I always daydream or wait until the last minute, and then it's too late.

Dad tops off his travel coffee mug. "Okay, we're off!" He bends down and messes up my hair.

"Dad, no!" I just spent five whole minutes trying to make it smooth. "Ugh!"

He laughs.

"It's not funny!" It's not like last year when I could just go to school and no one really paid any attention to my hair. Or did they? I never picked up on them noticing it then, but they do now. I don't need to give them another reason to laugh.

Mom nudges him and shakes her head the tiniest bit.

He clears his throat and says, "Sorry. See you this afternoon!"

"Mmm-hmm." I shovel a spoonful of cornflakes into my mouth, and they're out the door. I glance at the seat next to me. It's the one Maddie always sits in at breakfast after we have a sleepover. Last time, we stayed up late watching *The Greatest Showman* and my mom woke us up with pancakes. I think of Maddie saying that middle school scared her more than anything. My stomach gurgles, and I drop my spoon into my bowl. Why does everything have to remind me of her? I can't stop thinking about what I did.

This isn't who I am. With my heart pounding, I pick up the phone and dial Maddie's cell. It rings once. She's probably still at home. It rings a second time and goes to voice mail. I frown and hang up. Maddie *always* listens to music on her phone in the mornings, which means she saw me calling and sent it to voice mail. At least she knows that I called, but it's not enough. I scribble I'm sorry on a piece of paper and stick it into my pocket. I'm not sure this is enough, either, but I have to do something.

My eyes dart to the clock on the microwave, and I dump my dirty dishes into the sink before heading down the street to the bus stop. Lyric is already sitting by the curb, playing on her phone. Her perfectly polished aqua fingernails pop next to her deep brown skin. That color was always her favorite. It seems like forever ago that I used to paint her nails for her.

"Hey," I say quietly, just to see what she'll do.

She doesn't look up from the screen.

I drop my bag to the ground and plop down against it with a sigh. She wasn't like this in elementary school, when we all used to ride bikes together. But that was before her parents got divorced and she started spending half her time at a different house. Then she grew half a foot, and everything changed. At first, she said that she was too busy to play, or that it was too hot to go outside. It took me forever to realize that she didn't want to see *me* anymore. It's like she suddenly decided the rest of us were still little kids and she wasn't.

Maybe you just outgrow people. How does that even happen? Like, one day your friends are your friends, and the next, you're like a winter coat that's too small. So they donate it and leave it in the driveway for pickup, right where I'm sitting.

Every now and then Lyric absentmindedly pulls on curly strands dyed with really cool blue streaks at the end. The color almost matches her nails. She taps her phone a few times until it makes a whooshing sound.

I wish I had a phone so I could text Maddie. I asked my parents for one when school started, and Dad said, "We'll talk about it when you're in eighth grade." He might as well have said "never."

We both look up when we hear the engine chugging up the hill.

When the bus stops, I climb the steps and glance at my usual seat. Maddie isn't next to the window. Her bag is, and she's on the side closest to the aisle. My seat is gone. Did she see that I called? I drop the note onto her bag and wait for what feels like forever. She glances up at me, and then turns and looks out the window.

My heart aches. I swallow the lump in my throat and continue toward the back of the bus.

Lyric glances at me out of the corner of her eye when I sit near her. I look out the window and brace myself for the rest of the ride. Tristan and Josh lean over Maddie's seat again, and this time, the kid sitting in front of Maddie turns around and laughs with them.

I watch everything from the safety of the back of the bus, and when I can't take any more, I look out the window. What is it about middle school that changes everything—and everyone? It shouldn't be possible to destroy years of friendship in half a second, but I managed to do it. And I realize, amid the cruel laughter coming from behind her seat, that I've made the biggest mistake of my life.

I'm sitting in English as my eyes read the same lines over and over again. I have no clue what I'm reading. I can't concentrate on anything today—not since homeroom. Maddie had crumpled my apology note up into a ball and left it on my seat. But I guess I knew a simple "sorry" wouldn't work. And if that wasn't bad enough, Mr. Burton gave me another note that I definitely didn't want. It said:

> *Dear Charlotte,*
>
> *I missed you on Wednesday! Why don't you come chat during homeroom one day next week? Just tell Mr. Burton you need to go to the library, and he'll know! Can't wait to meet you!*
>
> *—Ms. Garrett*

I threw both notes into the trash.

"Time's up!" Ms. Harper says, moving to the front of the room. "Before we get started on anything else, I want to talk about our new project. Starting Monday, we're going to write every day."

I close my book.

"It can be funny or serious. It can be short. It can be long. It can be anything you want, as long as you just write *something*. Maybe you want to treat it like a daily journal, or you could write part of a short story every day. Whatever it is, it's okay. Just *write*. It can be fact or fiction. It can be fact you wish were fiction. It can even be facts that you turn into fiction!

"And it doesn't have to be perfect, either. What matters is that every day, we write something, just like we read something every day. Together. I'm going to write, too!"

I wonder what Ms. Harper writes about. . . .

"We're *all* going to be writers in here, and I can't wait to read your work."

I lean forward, and my chair squeaks. If she's going to read our work, we can't really write *anything*. So how do I decide what to write?

She looks around the room at each of us as she speaks. "You all have the potential to be"—she lands on me— "extraordinary." Deep in my bruised heart, a spark catches and pops out the dented places. Whatever I write, I'm going to make it the best thing I've ever written.

"If you want to be funny, go for it! If you want serious,

that's fine. Oh! For the artists in the room, if you want to tell your story in comic strips like they do in graphic novels, that's great." Ms. Harper's eyes light up as she talks about everything we can write.

"We can draw cartoons for this?" Ben asks.

"Of course you can!" Ms. Harper says. "Graphic novels are important books that tell stories, too."

"Awesome," the guy in front of me says.

"If you feel stuck coming up with ideas, try this: write what means something to you."

*Maddie.* But it's not like I can write about what happened if Ms. Harper is going to read our work. It's the worst thing I've ever done. I just . . . I don't want anyone to know. Especially Ms. Harper. My excitement fades.

"Questions?" She looks around. "No? Okay, time for lit circles!"

I can't imagine what she'd say if she read my story about the Bad Thing. I'd better tell another one.

At lunch, I open the paper sack that Mom surprised me with this morning. Folded up right on top of my peanut butter and jelly sandwich is a piece of paper. I smooth it out and read:

*Charlotte,*

*I hope you're having the best day! I'm so proud of the young lady you're becoming. Your kindness shows in everything you do. I love you!*

*Xoxo, Mom*

I grip the note in my hand. I'm not kind; I'm a coward! If she saw the real me, she wouldn't be leaving me lunch notes. Or lunches.

I was so busy trying to save myself that I made someone else feel bad. But that's not the kind of person I am. I have to do *something*. I tap the note against my juice carton.

Ben walks by my table with his tray. His missing hair looks even worse up close. He keeps his eyes on the floor and ends up at the next table. I wish there were some way to make him feel better.

I tap the note again and glance down at it.

I have an idea.

## CHAPTER EIGHT

# THE BIGGEST CHICKEN AT CAROL BURNETT MIDDLE

In social studies, I line up a piece of paper next to my notes so I can start thinking about another kind of note. I just have to wait for the right moment in class. We already worked in groups on our vocabulary words and had to illustrate each one and use it in a sentence. Now Ms. Yang wants each of us to take a turn reading the definition of a vocabulary word out loud and acting it out, and then the class has to guess the word. If we don't want to do it, all we have to do is say the magic word "pass," and the exercise moves to the next person. There's just one problem. *P* is a hard sound, and I can't start a sentence with it without stuttering. I can't read out loud without stuttering. I don't know why we can't just learn stuff without being embarrassed every five minutes.

"Pass."

"Pass."

"Pass." The line zooms closer to me. No one else wants to read, either.

"Pass."

"I'll read," a girl named Sophie says. Phew! Glancing up at Ms. Yang, I nod like I'm listening, and then I look down and write:

Dear Ben,

I tap the end of my pen against my chin. What do I say? I want him to know he has a friend, even if he never knows it's me. I like the idea of it being anonymous. I jot down:

Has anyone ever told you that you're awesome?

"Charlotte?"

"Yeah?" I look up, and everyone is staring at me. It's my turn. Maybe if I start with a soft sound first, I can get the words out. "Uh, p-pass." Ugh! I hate it, I hate it, I hate it. I sound like I'm searching for my words when I say "uh" like that, and it didn't even work this time. My cheeks burn, and even though they're already saying "pass" in the next row, my pulse continues to race. I glance around at the other kids with their open social studies books, sure that at least one of them noticed. But no one is even looking at me. They're all following along on the page like nothing happened.

I tug at my collar, glance down at Ben's note, and pick up my pen again. My mom's words echo in my head. *Your kindness shows in everything you do.* So I write:

> You're always nice to everyone, even if they don't treat you the same way. I think that's my favorite thing about you. I just wanted to tell you that you're not alone. I wish I were brave enough to say it out loud, but I'm not. But I wanted you to know it, so I'm writing this note.
>
> Your friend,

I stop. How should I sign it? I don't want to use my real name. It made me too nervous to do that when the principal asked me to write about the bus. But I felt safe to write the truth about the bus because the principal said it was secret. I don't know what it is, exactly, but there's something about being anonymous that lets you tell the truth, no matter what. So, for the first time all year, I own up to exactly who I am:

> The Biggest Chicken at Carol Burnett Middle

On the first day of musical theater, Ms. Harper told us that performing is all about presence, and she asked if we knew what it meant. Of course, no one really had any clue except for Aubrey, who squirmed and waved her arm around while Ms. Harper ignored her. When Ms. Harper finally called on her, Aubrey said, "It's when you're completely comfortable in front of everyone, and they love watching you."

Ms. Harper's mouth twitched. "Not quite, but I appreciate your enthusiasm. Anyone else?"

We sat there waiting for her to tell us.

"Presence is so many things. It's your voice, your posture, the way you command the room. But I think if you really want to have presence, you have to tell the truth." Ms. Harper smiled.

"And if you tell the truth as that character, if you *become* that character, you'll convince the audience to believe the lie, to suspend their disbelief. You're not really that character at all. They know that, but if you're good enough, you'll make them forget it. When they do, they won't be able to take their eyes away from the stage. *That* is presence."

I didn't know what she meant then, and I'm still not entirely sure what it means. All I know for sure is that I can't be afraid to speak if I want to command a room. Or a stage. I have to own my space, or at least make them think I do.

If I pretend to be brave long enough, will I *become* brave? Is that even possible? I wonder if that would work on the bus.

Ms. Harper gestures to a row of stacked pages. "These are the script audition pages for *The Wizard of Oz*. Take a few minutes to select the characters you'd like to read for so you can work on them this weekend. And don't forget your sheet music for your audition song."

That's all we need to hear. The whole class swarms over the pages.

I grab for the tray marked GLINDA at the same time as Aubrey. She does a double take when she realizes it's me, and stares like my hair is on fire. It's all over her face—she doesn't think I have what it takes. Aubrey can think whatever she wants, but since I have to audition anyway, I might as well go for Glinda.

"You're going to read for Glinda?" Aubrey says.

"Yep." I smile at her, trying to be friendly.

"Oh," she says. "That's . . . fun." Fun? *Fun!* What does she mean by that? It can't mean anything nice. "Just, you know, try not to be disappointed when you don't get the part."

My smile fades. Maybe it's Ms. Harper's speech about telling the truth, or maybe it's my note to Ben that makes me do what I do next.

I stand up straighter. I don't care if Aubrey *is* in a commercial. I'm in this class, too, and I can audition for what I want. I shrug and say, "We've all got a shot! That's why we audition. But thanks for saying that. And I hope *you* won't be upset if you don't get the part." And I say it *without* stuttering! Progress. No, wait. *Presence.*

Her jaw drops.

"G-good luck," I say, and head back to my seat with a smile on my face. I don't even care that I stuttered. Aubrey might be surprised next week. Maybe I'll even shock myself and have an awesome audition.

I keep my eyes on Ben's chunk of missing hair as I fight through the crowd on the way to the buses. When I go through the double doors of the bus, I catch up so I'm directly behind him. Three steps to go. It's now or never. My fingers curl around the note in my pocket, and I slip it into the gap between zippers on his bag by the time we reach the top step. He throws his bag into the first seat and slides in next to it. He doesn't even look at me.

Mission accomplished. Maybe I can still be the girl my mom wrote the note for this morning. A small smile crosses my face right as Maddie looks up at me. The disappointment in her eyes stops me in my tracks. Without a word, she turns and writes in her red notebook.

"Come ON! Keep moving," one of the eighth graders yells from the stairs.

I hurry past to an empty seat in the back.

Then before I know it, Josh and Tristan are seated across the aisle from Maddie. Why don't they just play with their phones or something? Maybe if she ignores them for long enough, they'll leave her alone. But that's not going to happen because Maddie will tell them off every time. It's just who she is, and they're having fun messing with her.

Tristan throws his hands up in the air and mimics Maddie telling him to stop.

A good person wouldn't let this happen. A good person would *say something.*

But I think I used up all my courage with Aubrey today. I look away and sink down lower in my seat.

## CHAPTER NINE

# AUDITIONS

On Saturday, Mom calls upstairs. "Charlotte! Dinner!"

"Just a minute," I yell. I replay the instrumental track for my audition song and sing the intro *one more time*. I'm getting better, but it has to be perfect if I'm going to prove I have the voice for Glinda in just sixteen bars. And then maybe, just maybe, everything else will be okay. Maybe I'll find my truth—and my voice—onstage. Maybe I'll figure out how to use that voice in school.

At the table, Dad says, "It's sounding good up there."

"Thanks," I say.

"Is anyone else reading for Glinda?" Mom asks.

"Yeah. Aubrey is. Maybe others. I don't know."

"Oh! Some of the elementary teachers were talking about her today. Isn't she the kid from the music video?" Dad asks.

My fork hovers halfway to my mouth. "No!" I hope she isn't. That just wouldn't be fair. How can I compete with a girl who has been in a commercial *and* a music video?

Mom leans in just a bit and gives me an encouraging smile. "You're going to do *fine*. You have a beautiful voice."

I half grimace/half smile in silence. "Unless I choke." What if I get so nervous that I can't sing at all? I prod at my meat loaf. Suddenly I'm not hungry anymore.

Mom pats my shoulder. "You're *not* going to choke! You just get up there and sing your heart out."

I nod. My stomach gurgles. If only I could stop thinking about auditions. I push away my plate. "Hey, Dad?"

"Hey, you."

"Do you really think I'm good enough to get cast?"

He looks at me over the rims of his dark glasses. "You put your pants on the same way they do, don't you?"

"Yeah, but do I *sing* like they do?"

"Better."

I frown. "Dad. Come on. I'm not a little kid."

"What? I gave you my opinion! Believe me, or don't. My answer isn't going to change."

And he looks so honest digging his fork into his mashed potatoes that I start to believe him.

I prep for the audition all day on Sunday. After breakfast, I grab my hairbrush and hold it like a magic wand, waving it around as I practice saying the lines to myself in my bedroom mirror. Over and over, I slowly say the words that begin with hard sounds. That's the part I'm most worried about. I don't stutter when I sing, but saying lines will be a whole different story. I know I'm going to be super nervous tomorrow, and whenever that happens, I get stuck more than usual. A line like "Did you forget the slippers?" becomes "D-d-d-did you forget the slippers?" Or Ms. Harper could ask me a question, and my brain might race too fast for my mouth to keep up. I'll get louder and faster, and then out of nowhere, my throat will tense and betray me. So, I practice sentences using easy onset like my old speech teacher taught me. I breathe in, I breathe out, and I slowly say the beginning of the word. It takes all morning, but I say the lines again and again until I can do it without stuttering. Sometimes if I know exactly what I'll be saying and I practice enough, I can get through it without stuttering as much. Sometimes I can't.

Mom makes me take a lunch break, and then we watch *The Wizard of Oz* while she runs lines with me. After the tenth run-through, Mom high-fives me and says, "I think you're ready."

I drop my script pages onto the coffee table. "I hope I can get through this tomorrow."

"You can do it, Charlotte. Just remember to breathe."

"I know, I know." I try not to roll my eyes. Mom is always reminding me to breathe, but at least she's not giving me silent hand signals anymore to remind me to slow down. After the elementary school suggested it, she did it all the time, no matter where we were. It just made me feel like . . . so much less. I know when I'm stuttering. I don't need anyone to draw *more* attention to it. This summer I told her how it made me feel, and she hasn't done it since. My mom is good like that.

When the movie ends, I go upstairs and practice my audition song with *and* without music, just in case something goes wrong. If I can just make the song perfect, maybe the rest won't matter.

But when I finally crawl into bed and all that stands between me and the stage is a few hours, the rest of my audition is all I can think about.

Monday passes in a blur, until finally the auditions are here. The house lights are on in the auditorium, lighting up the stage and the seating area. The piano is onstage, and right in front of the stage, there's a table with a few chairs.

"Let's get started!" Ms. Harper says. "But first, some

ground rules. You will hand your music to Ms. Bishop, and she'll play your selection for you. When you're finished, tell me the role or roles you're reading for, and I'll read opposite you. Everyone clear?"

We nod.

"These auditions are open, which means the rest of you will sit in the first two rows of the audience and observe. While your classmates are performing, there will be *no* talking. Please give them the same courtesy you would like to have while you're auditioning."

My stomach plummets. I was pretty sure it would be open, but deep in my heart I was still hoping I wouldn't have to audition in front of everyone.

"If you're uncomfortable with everyone watching, remember that the world will watch you sing onstage soon enough! This is good practice!"

*Get out of my head, Ms. Harper.*

"We'll go in order of the audition sign-up sheet. When someone is auditioning, I want the next person waiting to perform to stand offstage and be ready to go on. Questions?"

No one speaks. I think we're all terrified.

"Great. Break a leg! First up is Evie; second is Aubrey. Then we'll have Grace and Charlotte. Let's go, ladies." Ms. Harper sits at the table in front of the stage, clicks the end of her pen, and reaches for a clipboard. "Announce the song you're singing and the musical it's from, please."

Evie steps onto the stage and says, "I'm singing 'My New Philosophy' from *You're a Good Man, Charlie Brown.*"

I lean forward. That's a really hard song.

Evie throws back her auburn hair and sounds great until she messes up on the high note. She reads for the Wicked Witch, and her cackle is spot-on.

Two more auditions to go, and then it's my turn. I squirm in my seat.

"Grace! You're on deck. Aubrey, when you're ready."

Aubrey goes up onstage and says, "I'm going to sing 'That Would Be Enough' from *Hamilton.*"

Seriously? She can't sing *that*. That's an awesome song! Why didn't I think of it?

My heart starts to pound faster. It's almost my turn. I take a deep breath. I've got this. I practiced so hard. All I have to do is go up there and sing like I did in my room.

Ms. Bishop plays a few bars, and then Aubrey sings. Her voice is so pretty. I glance at my classmates. Everyone looks impressed. Jack is smiling toward the stage like he's just seen his first beach sunset.

I rest my chin in my hand. *Breathe, Charlotte.* They haven't heard me yet. I'm ready.

Then Aubrey pulls a pencil out of her back pocket and says she'll be reading for Glinda. *Please don't be perfect, please don't be perfect, please don't be perfect.* But of course she's perfect. Aubrey holds her pencil like it's a gorgeous wand and makes elegant sweeps of her arms while welcoming Dorothy to Munchkinland. She's not just auditioning—she's *loving* it. Before she even leaves the stage, I know she's going to get the part. I sigh. But in the back of my mind, I can still see myself as Glinda in my bedroom mirror.

"Thanks, Aubrey. Okay, Grace, you're up, and next on deck is Charlotte!"

I gulp. One more audition to go, and it's showtime. My stomach makes a sloshing sound. I grab my sheet music and walk toward the stage at the same time that Aubrey makes her way down the stairs. As we cross paths, she says, "Good luck beating that, sixth grader. *Hamilton* is Ms. Harper's favorite."

My jaw drops. It's fine. *Shake it off, Charlotte. She's just trying to mess with your head.*

Grace belts out "This Is Me" from *The Greatest Showman,* and by the time she's done, I'm blown away. That was awesome. She reads for Dorothy, and if I had a vote, it would be for her.

"Thanks, Grace! Okay, Charlotte, you're up!"

My mouth goes dry as I take quick steps toward Ms. Bishop to hand her the music. My heart is hammering so hard, everyone else must be able to hear it, too. Sweat starts to trickle down the back of my neck. Why is this happening? I've rehearsed this song so many times. I learned it backward and forward, and not once did I ever host a tropical rain forest in my armpits. I take a breath and look into the audience. "I'll be singing 'Something There' from *Beauty and the Beast*." I shouldn't have looked into the audience. They're all staring at me, especially Aubrey, and now there's so much adrenaline flowing that I can't think straight. But I have to sing, or they'll all see me for the chicken that I am. I take a deep breath.

The music starts, and I sing the best part of the whole song, when Belle belts out her feelings. My voice rings out, perfectly clear and filling the entire auditorium. It's just like I thought it would be. *I'm doing it!* I steal another glance at my class as I reach for the higher note, and I think, *What if I mess up?* A surge of panic hits me, and my voice cracks. It might as well be my heart. I gasp, which throws my carefully rehearsed breathing into all the wrong places. I can't keep up. I shut my eyes. The perfect song I planned is a mess. My heart thuds so hard, the beat moves to my head and I can't hear the music. Is that *my* voice? It's so far away, it doesn't even sound like it's coming from me. What am I even doing here? Who told me I could sing? Besides my parents. And let's face it, they don't count.

The blood rushes into my face, and I don't need a mirror to know that my cheeks and ears match the crimson stage curtains. This is not at all the way I pictured my audition. Finally the music ends, and I take a deep breath, trying to calm myself. Maybe the song wasn't too terrible. I'm supposed to say something right now, but I can't remember what it is.

Ms. Harper looks up from her clipboard. "And who are you reading for today?"

"G-G-G—" *Calm down and say it, Charlotte!* I look away so I don't see their faces, take another breath, and say, "Uh, Glinda." I smile through my panic. My throat tightens.

"Great! Ready when you are."

I try to picture myself in the role I've been thinking about all week, but it's no use. I'm wearing a shirt with wet armpit stains, the part of my audition that was supposed to be the best was a disaster, and there's nothing in all of Oz that can turn me into who I want to be. I focus super hard and try to get through my lines without messing up or getting hung up on a word, but I stutter again. And again.

I return to my seat, which is unfortunately way too close to Aubrey, and try to hold myself together while Ms. Harper calls the next kids to the stage. If only I hadn't had to audition in front of everyone and gotten so nervous, maybe it would have turned out differently. Who's going to cast me as anything after that?

I never realized how many girls are in this class compared to guys. I watch as girl after girl knocks it out of the park, and I feel worse by the second. When Sophie sings "Journey to the Past" from *Anastasia*, her voice squeaks on the second line, and her fair complexion turns scarlet. Everyone else sounds like they've had voice lessons compared to us.

I sit up straighter when Jack sings. I could listen to his voice all day. When he finishes reading for the Tin Man, he jogs down the steps and moves toward me. He grins, steps closer to my aisle, and just when I think he's going to say hi, passes right by me and approaches Aubrey. "You were great up there," he says to her.

*I* could've been great.

"Time for the dance portion," Ms. Harper announces. "Everyone onstage, please. Form three rows behind me." She stands in the center. Everyone rushes to be right behind her, and of course, I get stuck in the back. "Watch carefully and follow along." Ms. Bishop hits play from the sound booth, and "We're Off to See the Wizard" echoes across the empty auditorium.

Then Ms. Harper is moving, and the kids in front of me close in so much, I can't see her. I follow as best I can, but I have no clue how they're moving their feet.

"Okay, go again with me!" she says, nodding to Ms. Bishop to replay the music. And they're off. I move left, I move right. I throw my arms up when they do. Maybe I can fake it.

"Do you have it down?"

"Yes!" they say.

"Are you ready to make it count?"

"Yes!"

No. I need another month.

"Row one, stay where you are. Everyone else, sit out this round." She finishes scribbling something on her clipboard. "Okay, take it away!"

The music begins, and row one does a series of slides and hops, and even throws in a skip and a clap. I try to memorize it, but it's impossible, since I can't move with them. "Excellent job! Row one, please exit the stage. Row two, you're up!" They're not as good as row one, but they're way better than I am. Finally Ms. Harper says, "Row three, show me what you've got!" Not much. I shuffle across the stage, trying to keep up with everyone, and failing miserably. At least no one laughs.

Ms. Bishop cuts off the music.

"Thank you, row three!" Ms. Harper says as we return to our seats. "You were all outstanding today. I want you to give yourselves a big hand."

Everyone around me cheers and claps, but I just clap once.

"The cast list will be posted tomorrow by the beginning of class. I can't wait to get started!"

The bell rings, and as I'm picking up my backpack to leave, Grace says, "Hey, Charlotte."

I freeze. I'm not sure I can talk to anyone right now, so I answer without looking up. "Yeah?"

"You have a really nice voice. I love that song."

Now I have to look up. I search Grace's face for sarcasm as she tucks a stray corkscrew curl behind her ear, but I don't see any. I think she actually means it. "Thanks. I thought you were amazing."

Her dimples spotlight her smile. "Thanks."

We walk toward the door, and right as I break off to go to my bus, she says, "See you tomorrow!"

"Yeah, see you!" I say. And somehow, even after my terrible audition, I feel better.

When I climb onto the bus, I look up just in time to lock eyes with Ben in the first seat. He smiles at me. Does he know I gave him the note? Nah, he couldn't. But maybe the note *made* him smile. I grin back, and quickly move my eyes to the floor until I reach an empty seat closer to the back. I feel Maddie's eyes on me as I go.

I've always thought of myself as a good person. I never make fun of other people. I recycle plastic bottles to help save the planet. When I find a bug in the house, I don't squash it. I set it free outside. So, why can't I figure out how to do the right thing with Maddie?

I don't know if Maddie read my "I'm sorry" note before she crumpled it. She might not even *want* a note from me, but I could make her feel better with a secret note. If anyone needs one, it's her.

No, that won't work. She knows my handwriting, and she'll definitely realize it's me if I sign it "The Biggest Chicken . . ."

But I need to do *something* right. Something *good.*

I think about my tryout, and then I think about leaving the auditions with Grace. I take out a sheet of paper, and write:

> Dear Sophie,
>     I think it's really cool that you sang that song from <u>Anastasia</u>. It's a hard song and you were brave to sing it—way braver than I would be.
>                              —The Biggest Chicken at
>                              Carol Burnett Middle

It's not a big thing, but Sophie's voice cracked like mine. At least I can make someone feel less alone . . . even if it's not Maddie.

I go straight to my room when I get home, and I don't come out when I hear my parents arrive. I just burrow deeper under the covers and replay the disaster that was my audition.

There's a knock at my door. "Charlotte?"

"Mfff?"

Mom opens the door. "How did it go?"

I poke my head out from under my blanket. "Is it too late

to drop out of this class and take something else? Like study hall or something?"

"It couldn't have been that bad."

I sigh. "It kind of was."

She sits down next to me on the bed. "What happened?"

I tell her everything. How everyone else seemed to have it so together, and even though I practiced nonstop, I still choked when I stepped onstage. I feel the familiar heat moving into my face, and tell her about the moment I first stuttered, which is big for me because I never talk about that. I just like to move on and pretend it didn't happen. "Mom, I just . . . I wish I didn't stutter. You know? I hate it. I have all these things I want to do, and stuttering makes it so much harder."

She strokes my hair. "Have you met your new speech teacher yet?"

"No!" I push the covers back. "And I hope I don't, either. It's so stupid. They can't fix me, so why announce to everyone that I'm different?" I'm not going to grow out of stuttering. It's part of me, just like the freckles on my nose, except you can't always see it. I don't know how long I can keep ignoring Ms. Garrett. Sooner or later, she's going to send for me.

"No one's announcing anything."

"Oh yes, they are! We know when kids get called out of class. It's super obvious."

"I think you're paying way more attention to it than anyone else does. They're too busy worrying about what people are thinking about them."

Jeez, my mom is so old. She has no idea what middle school is really like. "Every time they take me out of class, I miss something important, or I get stuck with homework because everyone else gets to finish their work in class."

She shakes her head. "You have to give it a chance. It could help."

I scowl. "It won't. I don't know why the school makes us have meetings every year. I just want them to leave me alone!" Especially now. It always takes a few weeks at the beginning of the year before the speech teacher pulls me out of class. I have just enough time to feel like everyone else, and then it's like the universe says, *Not so fast, Charlotte Andrews!*

"I know you do. And when you're older, we can talk about whether you still need to meet with a speech teacher," Mom says. "But for now, I want you to keep trying the exercises to see if they can help you."

"Ugh. I wish I were already older. Or maybe just invisible."

"I don't believe that," Mom says.

I groan. "Why does everything have to be so hard? I just want . . ." I actually let myself say it. "I want to speak perfectly like everybody else. If I have to be onstage, I want to be *good* at it. Not like . . ." I bury my face in the pillow. *Me.* That's what I want to say.

She waits for me to finish. When I don't, she says, "It wouldn't be a dream if you didn't have to fight for it."

I prop myself up with my elbow and rest my chin in the palm of my hand. Several of the kids in my class have been in dance since they could walk. They've had voice lessons, they've done summer arts programs, and one of the eighth-grade girls can even twirl a baton when it's on fire. It's not that I didn't have the opportunity to do those same things. Every year, my mom asked if I wanted to sign up for an extra class, and I always said that I didn't want to. She never knew that I secretly did but I was too afraid to try. I didn't want to be made fun of. But saying no didn't work this year. My mom made me do musical theater anyway. So now I have to work twice as hard as everyone else to be half as good. I don't have any training, unless watching every musical under the sun counts. But I want to be good. I just don't know how to make it happen.

## CHAPTER TEN

# SECRET FRIENDS

I make a beeline straight to Ms. Harper's classroom, but there's no cast list on the door or the wall yet. I walk back toward homeroom. When I reach the bathrooms, Maddie turns from the water fountain. For the first time in forever, there's no one else around. It's just us, the way it used to be.

"Hi," I say.

She wipes her mouth on her sleeve and gapes at me. "*Hi? Are you kidding me, Charlotte?*"

I inwardly cringe, but I can't give up now. This could be my one chance to fix things. "I just wanted to say hi."

She rolls her eyes. "That's great. Thanks." Her words drip with sarcasm.

I want to make this right. I have to try. "You know I'm still your friend, right?"

"No."

I attempt a smile. "I am."

She stares at me with disgust. "Just leave me alone, Charlotte."

"Wait! I could sit with you again!" I search her face, desperate to fix this mess. I'll sit with her every day for the rest of middle school, if she'll just forgive me.

"No," she says, her eyes cold. "You can't."

I was right. I completely blew it. What do I do? "Okay, so if we don't talk on the bus, maybe we can still talk here in the hallway sometimes. If you want."

"You mean like secret friends?"

My mouth drops open. I didn't dream she'd ever be embarrassed by me. "You don't want to talk to me anymore?"

The moment the words leave my mouth, Maddie's eyes flash with anger.

"I never said that, Charlotte! You're the one— Did you actually think I'd—" She sighs. "You're such a coward. It's like you're afraid of me or something."

I'm not afraid of her. But actually, right now at this moment, she's a little scary. "I am not."

"Please. You're the biggest chicken in the whole school."

My jaw drops. I thought I was the only one who knew that.

She tilts her head. "And you know it. I feel sorry for you."

"You—I mean—you feel sorry for me?"

She shakes her head. "Better go before someone sees you with me. Since we're secret friends and all."

"Maddie, I—"

She turns and walks away.

By the time I get to homeroom, Maddie is already reading a book at her desk, and I walk past her like we were never friends at all. It's so weird how one little thing can erase what you are to someone. I mean, I guess it wasn't so little. It was a big thing, a *bad* thing, and I did it without even thinking about it. And then *poof,* I was erased.

No. I did the erasing. And now I can't take it back.

Mr. Burton walks over to my desk and hands me an envelope with familiar handwriting on it. "Hey, Charlotte, this came for you."

"Thanks," I mutter. This time, there's a cartoon sticker of a hedgehog wearing a top hat next to my name. I rip through the envelope and pull out the note.

> *Dear Charlotte,*
>
>     *I'm sorry we keep missing each other! I was sick last week and couldn't be at school like I'd planned. But don't worry—I'm going to pull you out of class soon so we can get to know each other and discuss your goals. Looking forward to meeting you!*
>
>                     *—Ms. Garrett*

I close my eyes and rest my head on my desk. Why does this have to happen now? Someday I won't be in middle school anymore. I won't have to do things that make me different. I can just be Charlotte. I sigh. What would that even be like?

At lunch, the line barely inches along while I hold my tray. It's supposed to be grilled cheese, but the bread is hard to the touch and the cheese looks like plastic.

Tristan and Josh are in line ahead of me because today wants to go down in history as awful. I hang back enough that they don't speak to me, but I can still hear what they're saying.

Josh says, "I'm just so tired from all the travel games. And have you seen the practice schedule for next week?"

"Tell him you need a break."

Josh lets out a bitter laugh. "Yeah. Try doing that when your dad's the coach."

The line moves forward.

Josh grabs a drink from the cooler. "Want to come over tonight and watch our plays from the game?"

Tristan sighs. "I can't. My dad has to work late and I have to watch my little brother."

I look up. I didn't know he had a brother. Or that he couldn't do everything he wanted to do.

"Oh, okay. Next time," Josh says. He pays for his sports drink and leaves.

Tristan enters his code at the register.

"Hold on a second," says the cafeteria lady. "Young man, your account is in the negative. You've maxed out the most you can owe."

Tristan runs his hand along the back of his neck. "Can't I pay you tomorrow?"

I try not to listen, but I can't help it. I've never seen Tristan look embarrassed before. Ever.

She raises her eyebrows into her hairnet. "No, but you can put that pizza down and have a peanut butter sandwich instead. No charge for that."

I guess he can't control everything in his life, either. Like I can't always control my speech. Like Maddie can't magically make everything better for everyone, even though she wants to. Being totally helpless is one of the worst feelings in the world, and I hate seeing anyone that way. Even Tristan.

He digs through his pockets. "Hang on."

The cafeteria lady purses her lips.

I feel so bad for him. But what am I supposed to do? Help him? I frown. If he knew I didn't have lunch money, he'd probably eat a candy bar in slow motion just to make me miserable. He'd never do anything to help me.

She sighs. "Come on, hon. Just take a sandwich. You're holding up the line."

Tristan shifts his weight, his face scarlet. He steals a glance over his shoulder at the long line behind him, his eyes full of worry.

I reach into my pocket and pull out a few dollars from my lunch-money stash. It doesn't matter what Tristan would do. I don't have to be like him. I get to choose to be kind. Taking a deep breath, I brace myself and tap his shoulder.

He whirls around, his eyes wide. "What?" he snaps, his voice higher than usual.

I hand him the money without a word. He can't make fun of my stutter if I don't speak.

"Uh, thanks," Tristan mutters. He sneaks a glance at my face, like he isn't sure what else to say, and then he bolts to a nearby table.

After I pay for my own lunch, I feel his eyes follow me all the way to my usual seat by the trash can. I glance over my shoulder.

He quickly looks away.

I keep checking outside Ms. Harper's door in between every class, and finally catch her taping a list to the wall right before musical theater. She slips back through the door, and the whole class pushes forward to find our names.

Grace shrieks. "DOROTHY!" She covers her mouth with her hands, and I think she's going to cry. "I can't believe it!"

An eighth-grade guy turns around and high-fives Jack. "Hey, Tin Man!"

With my heart pumping overtime, I burrow into the throng of kids and fight my way to the cast list. I place my finger at the top of the list and scan it all the way down. There are so many parts. There are even understudies for the main characters. I'm not any of those, though. *Oh, please let me be cast as something. Let me be cast—* And there's my name! I'm ON THE LIST! I take a deep breath and follow to the next line, where it says, "Apple Tree #1" and "Horse 2/2." My mouth drops open. Honestly, I'm happy I got a part. But a *tree*? Really? And what is this horse role?

Aubrey pushes to the front, finds her name, and turns around with the biggest smile on her face. "I'm Glinda! I knew it!"

Jack smiles at her and says, "You're going to be an amazing Glinda."

I turn to walk into the classroom. Some of the seventh graders follow behind me, their conversations peppered with excitement.

The bell rings. "Okay, everyone," Ms. Harper says. "Now that you know your roles, welcome to *The Wizard of Oz*!" She picks up a huge stack of papers. "I'm passing out your copies of the script. Take a few minutes to look it over. Today we're going to do our first read-through, minus the musical numbers!"

I open my copy and flip through the pages as quickly as I can. I finally find Apple Tree #1 in the pages right before Dorothy and the Scarecrow find the Tin Man. I actually have lines!

But where is the horse? Maybe there was one in Munchkinland that I missed? Or is it the one in the Emerald City that changes colors?

Ms. Harper clears her throat. "Okay, now that you've familiarized yourself with the script, let's put our desks in a big circle and go through it together! Try to read it in character and make it come to life. Get a feel for how it sounds when all the scenes are connected."

We screech our desks across the floor. Looking around, I realize that there are so many kids that I really don't know yet. I'm next to Sophie, who's also been cast as a horse. Her straight, white-blond hair falls across her face as she settles into her chair, so I can't tell if she's disappointed or just quiet. I wish I could find some way to slip the note I wrote for her into her bag, but she placed it too far away. So I fold the note and drop it near her foot when she isn't looking. I'm so smooth. She'll never know it was me!

We begin the read-through, and before I know it, we're on the page where Apple Tree #1 starts throwing apples at

Dorothy. I take a calming breath and read my lines. I only stutter once. But no one laughs. I sneak a peek at their faces, and they're all looking at their scripts, eyebrows furrowed in concentration, some of them smiling at the funny parts. Maybe this class isn't like everywhere else. I rest my chin in my hand. I may have a different kind of role, but I'm still part of the play. And every part is important.

Even being a horse isn't going to be that bad. All I have to do is walk offstage when someone says, "That's a horse of a different color." Sounds easy enough. No lines. Just exit stage left. I can do that.

That's it. I don't know what I was expecting, but this seems really simple. What could go wrong?

When the bell rings, Sophie bends down to pick up her band instrument case and scoops up my note without unfolding it. I watch her out of the corner of my eye as she strides to the back of the room and tosses the note into the recycling bin. I sigh. At least I tried.

In the evening, Mom and I walk down the grocery aisle picking out soft drinks to go with the pizza we ordered.

"Honestly," she says. "I think it's great! You're going to be amazing."

I grin. Maybe I could be.

We round the cereal aisle on the way to the checkout and almost collide with Maddie and her mom.

"Well, hello there!" Mom says.

Maddie stares at me without speaking, her face totally blank.

"Hi," Maddie's mom says with a smile.

Mom glances at me, and then at Maddie. The silence between us is so awkward, I can almost reach out and touch it.

"We're just picking up a few things to celebrate. Charlotte got cast in the musical!"

Maddie's mom says, "That's great!" There's a hint of sadness in her eyes when she looks at me, as though she's disappointed. Almost like . . . she knows everything I've done.

My heart leaps into my throat. Is she going to tell my mom? Is Maddie? They could do it right here.

Maddie says nothing.

Mom says, "It's too bad Maddie can't come with us to see *Wicked*!"

I gulp. My lie is out. We're nowhere near the frozen foods, but it feels like the temperature just fell twenty degrees.

Maddie's jaw drops. She quickly recovers with a shake of her head and narrowed eyes. She's never going to forgive me now. How do I keep making this worse? It's like the Bad Thing keeps getting bigger.

Her mother gives Maddie's shoulder a light squeeze. "Oh?"

"Well, yeah." Mom stares at me with raised eyebrows. "Isn't that what you said, Charlotte?"

Maddie and her mom turn to me.

My pulse quickens. If Maddie seemed mad this morning, it was nothing compared to now. I'm not getting out of this alive. Not a chance. "I, um . . . yeah. Some k-k-kind of family thing."

I look into Maddie's eyes. She can do anything she wants right now. She can tell them I'm lying, tell my mom about the bus, whatever. I can take it. It might feel good to just confess everything.

Almost mechanically, Maddie breaks into a forced smile and says, "Maybe next time. Thanks for the invite, Mrs. Andrews."

I release a sigh of relief. And just as quickly, I'm confused. Maddie actually covered for me after what I did? I search her face for answers. What does it mean? I don't deserve it, but maybe she hasn't completely given up on me and our friendship?

Mom studies us, sensing that something isn't quite right, but she can't put her finger on it. "Of course. You'll have to come over again soon. We haven't seen you in a while!"

Maddie's mom nods. "We haven't seen Charlotte lately, either. You know you're welcome anytime!" Her eyes meet mine, and there's not a doubt left in my mind. She knows.

We mutter our awkward goodbyes. As soon as we're in the parking lot, Mom says, "Charlotte, *what* is going on with you two?"

*Tell her, you big chicken.* I shrug. "It's nothing." *I ditched Maddie, and now she's really upset and probably hates me, but no, nothing's going on. We're all good here.*

"It seemed like something to me. You know," she says while she buckles her seat belt, "you two have been good friends for a long time. It would be a shame to let something come between you."

I stare down at my feet. I feel hollow, like a chocolate bunny without insides. I don't want things to be this way. I want to pick up the phone and tell Maddie how sorry I am, but if she wouldn't talk to me before, there's no way she'll talk to me now.

When we get home, I start to set the table, and Mom says casually, "Why don't we invite Maddie to go to a movie this weekend?"

I freeze, the plates forgotten in my hands. What do I say? "Uh, I'm going to be busy practicing for the play." *Please let that be a good enough excuse.*

Mom takes the plates from me and sets them on the

counter next to the pizza. "You're not going to be *that* busy." Her gaze practically cuts me.

I look away.

"Charlotte, what happened?"

I open the pizza box and study the pepperoni slices. "Nothing."

"That wasn't nothing at the grocery store. You can tell me, you know."

My shoulders fall. I can't ever tell her. She'd be so disappointed in me.

"Did you have a fight?"

I shrug.

"What was it about? Did Maddie say something that hurt you?"

I shake my head.

She sighs. "Charlotte."

"Yeah, Mom," I say, steeling myself for more questions.

"I'm right here." She squeezes my arm. "Whatever it is, I'm sure you can fix it."

My heartbeat quickens. I *can't* fix it. That's the problem. Some things are just too big. "I, um, okay."

"To be continued," she says with a wink as she helps herself to pizza. "But only because I'm hungry. One way or another, I'm going to get to the bottom of this!"

I gulp. My mom always keeps her promises. I grab a slice

of pizza and walk into the den right as a car commercial plays on the TV. I shriek and point to the screen, shaking my finger as Aubrey says, "Gee, Dad, look at all the legroom!" Then her TV dad shakes the car dealer's hand and says, "We'll take it." Aubrey doesn't even get out of the car. The screen zooms in until her smiling face is all that we see, and right when I think it can't get cheesier, a big cartoon sparkle appears in her right eye.

I put down my pizza.

"Isn't that the girl from the music video?" Dad asks from his recliner.

"No! She's *not* in a music video!" Is she?

"Which part did she get in the musical?" Mom asks.

I sigh. "Glinda." I guess that's a good thing—I'd be too nervous anyway.

Mom pats my shoulder. "She's been doing this way longer than you."

I shrug. "It's fine. Whatever." I peek over at Dad. "You're the best dad in the whole world. Did anyone ever tell you that?"

Dad laughs, making the skin around his eyes crease. "Out with it. What do you want?"

"What makes you think I want something?" I open my eyes super wide and hope I look innocent.

He tilts his head and waits.

"I was just thinking, since you're the best dad and all, that we could watch *The Wizard of Oz*."

*"Again?"*

"Please?"

He hands over the remote. "Go ahead," he says, padding into the kitchen for pizza.

"Yes!"

We all watch the movie for the millionth time. When Dorothy picks apples in Oz, I pay close attention to the trees. I wonder how you go to the bathroom in a costume like that.

## CHAPTER ELEVEN

# THE BEGINNING OF THE END

I kind of thought that Ms. Harper wouldn't read our writing project until report cards are due, but today when I pull my journal off the shelf, I flip to the last page, where I wrote about how the beauty of lightning bugs gets them crushed by kids who want to catch them. There's a note just for me in the margin. It says, *Very nice, Charlotte, but does it mean anything to you? What's something you really care about?*

Well, duh. How about how I'm only in musical theater because my parents made me, and I stutter, which makes everything harder, and I thought I could be good enough to play Glinda but . . . I'm not. But I can't write about that because she did the casting and I don't want her to think I'm mad. And I care a lot about Maddie, but I can't fess up to that, either. So I guess I'll be the weird kid writing about lightning bugs because everything real is off-limits.

I write back in the margin, I don't know yet. And I write a new story about a sock that gets lost, and no matter what it does, it can't get back to where it was. It's trapped in another dimension! While there, it has to relive every step starting from the moment it got lost, but it never gets to find out *where* the portal is. (It's in the dryer! Ha ha!) Every time it's about to get the answer, it goes all the way back to the beginning. At the top, I write: Where Missing Socks Go. There. That's creative. And I care about socks. They're important for foot hygiene. What's not to like?

Somehow, though, I don't think Ms. Harper wants a goofy story about missing socks.

When musical theater rolls around, Ms. Harper says, "Hi, everyone. I've just received a bit of news today, and I've asked to be the one to tell you." She sighs. "This will be the last year that musical theater is offered as a class."

The room immediately buzzes. Musical theater is a big deal here. Our school wins awards for it.

"But why?"

"We've always had musical theater!"

"That's not right!"

She holds up her hand for silence. "The school is going in a new direction. Next year we will have to use this time for enrichment reading classes."

"I'll bet it's because of our test scores!" someone blurts out near the back.

Grace says, "Yeah, I think my cousin's school made them do that when their scores dropped."

Ms. Harper clears her throat. "Regardless of the reason, this class won't be offered again. So, let's make the most of our time together and put on the best production this school has ever seen!"

I slump in my seat. This can't be it. I glance over at Aubrey, who looks like she's about to cry. I feel that way, too.

We work on the first few scenes for the rest of class. When the bell rings, I hang behind.

"Everything okay, Charlotte?" Ms. Harper asks from the door.

I fiddle with the zipper on my bag as I approach her. "It's just . . . Isn't there something we can do to save musical theater?"

Her face softens. "I wish. It would take a miracle to change it."

I shove my hands into my pockets and push my toe into the floor. "D-don't you believe in miracles, Ms. Harper?"

She smiles down at me. "I do."

"Me too."

She glances at the clock on her wall. "And unless you leave right now, you're going to need one to make it to your bus in time."

I gasp and run out the door as fast as I can. I only stayed an extra minute or two, so maybe it's not too bad.

But it *is* that bad—there's no one else around except for some older teacher who yells after me to slow down. I tear through the hallway, my backpack thumping hard against my shoulders. I have to make it, or I'm going to be in so much trouble! The double doors are just ahead. I push them open with the full force of my run behind me, and there's my bus, still there. I keep running and make it barely in time. I breathe a sigh of relief. And now I don't know where to sit. All of the seats at the back will be full. Ben sits to my left in the first seat. I glance back at Maddie, who crosses her arms over her red notebook and stares at me. Turning to Ben, I say, "Can I sit with you?"

He raises his eyebrows in surprise. "Sure." He swings his backpack onto the floor.

I slide into the seat and breathe big, raspy breaths. Sweat trickles down my neck.

The bus driver closes the doors and pulls away from the curb.

"That was close," Ben says.

"Yeah." I smile at him, and I realize I'm a much easier target in this seat, and the only good thing about sitting here is that it's right next to the bus driver. I want to check how close Tristan and Josh are sitting. Are they still behind Maddie? Or maybe next to her? I didn't notice, and I don't want to turn around to look. It's better if I don't know where they are.

The windows are slightly cracked, allowing the hot breeze to lift the stray pieces of my hair and wave them around. I gather my hair in my hand and hold it in place behind my neck.

Ben pulls a pencil out of his pocket and starts doodling in a notebook.

I run through a mental list of things I can't say.

*Hey, sorry about your hair.*

*I told the truth.*

"I haven't talked to you in forever," he says.

It would be a lot more accurate if he said *I* haven't talked to *him* in forever. The last time was two years ago, when we were in fourth-grade book club together and things weren't so weird. Our group met in the library on Friday mornings before school. It was awesome. I didn't avoid him on purpose then. "What are you drawing?"

"An alien encounter."

I lean closer to his notebook. "Wait, is that supposed to be you?"

"Yep. It's for Ms. Harper's class." All these snail-like creatures are surrounding a cartoon version of Ben, shaking his hands and smiling. He was always so good at art. Sometimes he'd draw scenes to go along with the books we read.

"What's that about?" I remove my glasses, wipe the smudges off with my shirt hem, and put them back on.

"This is where they're telling me that I'm really one of them, and they've come to get me," Ben says.

A laugh bubbles up in my throat, but something makes me hold it in. I don't want him to think I'm making fun of him.

He looks up from his drawing. "Don't you ever feel like that?"

"Like an alien? No."

"That's not what I mean. More like you're pretty sure you belong somewhere, and all you know is that it isn't here." He draws a top hat on an alien and adds some tentacles.

I stiffen. "Sometimes." Or every moment of my life, but who's counting? I wish I could tell him the truth— something real. Or do *something* besides just sit here. I think I have some candy stashed away. I reach into my backpack pocket and grab a pack of mints. Gum isn't even allowed at our school.

"I think your drawing is really good." I sit up and offer the mints.

He smiles and takes one. "Thanks. You think Ms. Harper will like it?"

"Oh, yeah," I say. "What's not to like?" It means something to him, plus he's a really good artist. She'll love it.

"I, um. I think I want to see if I can keep it going," he says.

"What do you mean? Like a book?"

"Maybe," he says. "I'd like to try it as a comic strip, and then see if I can make it longer."

"You should totally do it," I say without hesitation. Ben makes it look so easy.

I want to show Ms. Harper that I'm serious about writing, but it's harder than I thought it would be. I have to think of something good to write about, and soon.

## CHAPTER TWELVE

# IT'S NOT FAIR

In English class a few days later, I flip to the last entry in my notebook and find Ms. Harper's handwriting. *Compelling!* it says. I grin. I had heard two girls arguing in the hallway before class, so I imagined what would happen next and wrote about it. Below that line, it says, *But I wonder what's important to you, Charlotte?*

I tap the pen against my cheek. How do I tell the truth without saying what's actually happening? If I write something real, Ms. Harper will know *everything*. That can't happen. But I can't just ignore her question, so I answer by writing below it: Broken things that can't be fixed. Like my friendship with Maddie. For the millionth time, I wish I'd had the courage to speak up. What if I write about that without actually talking about the bus? It's important, and I think Ms. Harper will think so, too. I turn the page and write about why you should use your voice to stand up for what you believe in. If you don't speak up, no one will ever hear your voice. And you have a voice!

I glance at Ms. Harper scribbling away at her desk, and I wonder what's important enough for her to write about. All around the room, bookshelves are bursting with novels, and the walls are dotted with special issues of the school newspaper (she's the faculty sponsor) and Broadway musical posters. If I were her, I'd probably write about how unfair it is that she won't be able to teach musical theater anymore.

I think everyone was pretty upset about that, especially Aubrey. She was heartbroken, and honestly, I still feel bad for her. Maybe she could use some kind words. I know I could. I pull out a clean piece of paper and write:

Dear Aubrey,
    I'm so sorry about musical theater. I know how much it means to you.

I pause. It's so hard to give her a compliment when she was horrible about me trying out for Glinda. But this is about making her feel better, not my hurt feelings. Even if it's hard to say, I know that I still have to be kind. I swallow my pride and write:

You're going to shine as Glinda.

It's finally time for musical theater. Today we meet in the chorus room. I wasn't sure about performing in the beginning, but now . . . I kind of like it. I won't admit it to my parents, because they *made* me take this class, but I love the music. I love the story. And now I'm secretly disappointed because I know I'll never be able to take musical theater again at this school. I wish things could be different.

I wait until Aubrey drops her bag in the corner and joins some of the older girls laughing together in the center of the room. After I glance around to make sure no one is watching, I place Aubrey's note on her bag where she'll see it. The bell rings, and we sing all the songs while Ms. Bishop plays the piano. Ms. Harper says it will be easier for us to stage the songs if we already know the music. I love every minute of it.

"Ahem!" says Ms. Harper. "I have an important announcement. It's come to my attention that one of you has some very special news. Aubrey, would you like to share?"

Aubrey fans herself like she's embarrassed, but she's smiling so big that her face might crack. Or at least her makeup will. I'm not even allowed to wear makeup yet, and she looks like she robbed a Sephora.

Ms. Harper says, "Oh, it's okay! We're all friends here!"

Aubrey blushes. "I don't know. . . ."

"If you don't tell them, I will!" Ms. Harper winks at her.

Aubrey smiles and says, "Okay, this is so weird, but I'm going to be in a music video for—"

"DOLLY PARTON!" Ms. Harper yells.

My jaw drops while the rest of the class erupts into cheers. Are you kidding me? Dolly Parton? I thought Aubrey was still crushed over musical theater being canceled, but she has to be doing fine now. I glance back at her note. Oh well. I tried to do something nice. Maybe it will still do some good.

The classroom phone rings. Ms. Bishop answers. After a moment, she says, "I'll tell her." Ms. Bishop calls out, "Charlotte, they need you in the library!"

Everyone turns and stares. Oh my gosh, no. Not now. Can this day get any worse?

I grab my bag and dart out the door. The only good thing is that they didn't call me to the office, so I know I can't be in trouble. But honestly, it's going to be worse.

The library is full of kids working at computers. I stand there for a minute, looking around, until I see a woman waving at me through an open door.

I walk quickly to the back before anyone else sees her waving, and brace myself.

The woman in the doorway is probably around my mom's age, with sleek, dark hair and olive skin. "Hi, Charlotte! At last we meet! I'm Ms. Garrett, and we'll be working on your speech together this year." She holds her arm out as if to welcome me into her office, making her bracelets jingle and dance against her wrist.

I duck into the tiny room. All I wanted was to be like everyone else and get to stay in classes I actually like. Why do I always miss the best stuff? It's so wrong.

She shuts the door and beams at me. "Make yourself comfortable. Have a seat!"

I sink down into the cracked plastic chair in front of her desk.

Ms. Garrett sits down at her desk and smiles. "Now, I've been going over your files, and it looks like you've been making progress with some strategies."

If she means I've been forced to do this for years and have gotten stickers but nothing has ever changed, then yeah. I guess so.

"I see that one of the things your past speech teachers wanted you to do was 'cloud talk,'" Ms. Garrett says, reaching for a pen and marking something on a piece of paper.

"Yeah. In *kindergarten*," I reply.

"I think it's a great strategy at any age." She smiles, and the skin around her green eyes wrinkles just a bit. "Make your words light and fluffy, and you can pass from one to another."

Words aren't light and fluffy. They're hard, heavy, and unforgiving. They hurt people.

I sigh.

"I thought maybe you could read aloud from one of your textbooks," Ms. Garrett says. "Maybe something you need to study? We can continue practicing sentences using easy onset."

She means practicing sentences that start with harder sounds, like *K, G, P,* and *B*—the worst ones in the whole world—and taking a deep breath right before saying them. Then I'm supposed to slowly say the beginning of the word while breathing out. I give her the longest, biggest eye roll in the history of middle school. NO. I'm not reading my textbook. And I'm missing my favorite class so I can sit in here and talk about clouds. Why can't she take me out of something I don't enjoy? Like PE? It isn't fair. "I do that in class. I don't need to do it here."

"Will you try it?"

I don't move.

"For me?"

For *her*? I don't even know her. I'd do it for Ms. Harper in a heartbeat, though. "No, thank you."

"What about if we practice making phone calls?" She gestures at a play phone on her bookshelf.

I stare at her without smiling. Preschoolers play with toy phones, not middle schoolers. I already feel so small. That would just make it worse.

"What's your favorite class?"

"Musical theater. We're doing *The Wizard of Oz*."

"Oh, I love that musical!"

*Yeah, me too. Which is why I should be there now instead of in this cramped closet disguised as an office.* She's managed to cram a desk, herself, two chairs, and a tiny bookshelf in here, but I don't think anything else will fit.

"Do you know your lines yet?"

I try to play it off like I don't care about it. "Yeah. But I only have a few. I'm a tree and a horse."

"Really?" She tilts her head. "I would've totally seen you as Glinda."

I give her a withering look. It's like she *knows* I screwed up my audition.

She adds, "Or maybe the Wicked Witch. You could do that for sure."

The corners of my mouth twitch. At least she has a sense of humor. I'd laugh, but I'm not giving in just yet. She has to work for it.

"I have an idea. So you don't have many lines. Fine. But I'll bet you know everyone else's."

Yeah, I do. I memorized most of the script over the weekend. I shrug.

"What if we read from the script in here?"

*I'm listening* . . . but I glance off into the dusty corner like I'm not the least bit interested.

"You play the main characters, and I'll read against you. We can work on your goals that way. Oh, and this is very important—I want you to look me in the eye when you say the lines. We need to work on keeping good eye contact. Do you have the script with you?"

I want to hate everything she suggests, but this actually sounds fun. "Yeah."

"Great! Let's get started." She moves stacks of papers aside.

"Hey, Ms., um—"

"Garrett. But you can call me Ms. G."

"Yeah, Ms. G. Do you think next time you could get me out of a class I don't need?" I rummage in my bag for the script.

"Hmm, let's see." She pulls up my schedule. "I really don't want to get you out of one of your core subjects."

I sit up straighter. "But this is important! Right now I'm missing song rehearsal, and pretty soon we're going to start blocking and learning choreography. I should be there. People are counting on me." I place the script on her desk and give her a winning smile. "I was thinking I really don't need PE."

"Is that so?" She takes a sip from her coffee mug.

"Yeah. It makes me sweaty and gross, and if you get me out of PE, I won't stink up your office. Everybody wins!"

She chokes on her coffee.

I wait for her to stop coughing. "B-besides, I'll get plenty of exercise onstage. That should count for something."

"We'll see."

I slump in my seat. It was worth a try at least.

She turns the script sideways so we can both see it. "Ready when you are."

I sigh. If I had a choice, I'd never be ready for this. Even for a play as awesome as this one. "Where do you want me to start?"

"At the beginning. Where else?"

## CHAPTER THIRTEEN

# THE FIRST SPARKS

One week later, Mom's curled up on the sofa grading papers, with a jar of trail mix on one side of her and a pencil pouch full of stickers and different-colored pens on the other. I fall onto the other couch and cover up with the blanket that she keeps on the back of the cushions.

"Finish your homework?" she says.

"Yeah. . . . Hey, Mom?"

"Mmm?"

"I'm not okay with them canceling musical theater."

She gives me a wry smile. "They don't need your permission, hon."

"I know. I just . . ." I finally decided that the class isn't so bad, and they're just going to take it away? "I don't think they should. I want to stop them."

She peers over the top of her stack of student papers. "Them?"

"Mr. Sinclair and everyone who thought that canceling musical theater was a great idea. It's too important to all the kids in my class. The school can't just get rid of it." I'm going to be an awesome tree and a horse, but someday I might have even bigger roles! I want the chance.

She puts down her blue grading pen. "I don't know that you can do anything about it."

"I know I'm just a kid, and that means no one listens to me, but there has to be *something* I can do!"

She shakes her head. "Charlotte, people listen to you!"

I give her a look. "Do not."

"They do! *I* listen to you."

I sigh. "But you're my mom. You don't count!"

She gasps and clutches her hand to her heart like she's deeply wounded. "I beg your pardon!"

"Sorry," I say quickly. "I just . . . I need other adults to listen, too."

She settles back into the couch and studies me for a moment. "This means a lot to you, doesn't it?"

I nod.

Mom tucks the graded papers into her tote bag. "Then

make sure your voice is heard by someone who can do something about it. Tell your truth. Tell it loudly. If people don't listen, say it louder."

My shoulders fall. I've been so bad at speaking up when it's important. And now that I have a chance to do it again, I don't think it will do any good to talk to Mr. Sinclair. "But the principal isn't going to listen to us!" I frown. If I can even get the words out. Unless . . . I don't have to say them. I can write them!

"Who said anything about the principal? Think about it for a minute." She settles back into the couch.

It hits me. "Wait, you mean like the principal's boss?"

She smiles. "But why stop there?"

The next day, musical theater moves into the auditorium so we can do our blocking on the stage. All of our rehearsals will be here from now on.

We go through the play one scene at a time, running the lines as we go and learning where we're supposed to be. I have to yell at Dorothy in the big scene when she starts picking apples out of the trees, but it's so hard. It's one thing just to know the words and say them without stuttering, but now I have to *mean* them, too. It's not going well. I'm pretty much just shouting my lines into the auditorium.

Grace tries to keep a straight face, and says, "I'm sorry, but you're like the nicest person ever. You can't yell at me! It's just too much!"

I am *not* the nicest person ever. She has no idea.

Ms. Harper says, "Oh, but she's going to yell at you!" She turns to me. "Move a bit more to your left."

I do.

"Great. That's your new mark. You need to be standing there every time, and *mean it* when you say the lines. Got it?"

I nod.

"Okay, let's take it back to Dorothy picking the apple. Once more, with feeling. Get her, Charlotte!"

I can do this. I know it.

Dorothy reaches up for the imaginary apple, and this time when I yell, "Hands off my apples!" she doesn't laugh. We'd look a lot cooler if we were actually in costume, but our fitting isn't until next week.

When we finish the scene, some of the kids in the audience clap and smile. Grace gives me a fist bump and says, "That was awesome! Remind me not to tick you off."

I laugh. I actually *did* it. I yelled and hit my mark. And I meant it.

For the first time in my life, I feel like I'm actually part of something.

Ms. Harper checks her watch. "We don't have time to block another scene today. Go ahead and pair off with a friend. I'd like you to run lines with each other for tomorrow's scenes. Remember, the goal is to be completely off-book by next week! Tell the truth and make it count—this is going to be our very last show!"

Grace is already walking off the stage with Jack, but Sophie, aka Apple Tree #2, says to me, "Hey, you want to read with me?"

"Sure." We sit down in two of the auditorium seats near Grace and Jack. "Hey," I say. "Have you ever done a play before?"

"Nope. I guess I'm trying something new."

"Same," I say. "My parents kinda talked me into it. But I've always loved musicals."

Sophie smiles. "It's just not fair that they're ditching it our very first year. I can't believe this is it."

It's super quiet back here, but I don't care. I'm saying it anyway. "I was thinking, though—what if it doesn't have to be?"

She looks at me funny. "But it is. Ms. Harper said."

"Yeah, I remember. But maybe she didn't think of everything."

Grace turns around and drapes her arm over the back of her seat. Jack even glances in my direction. They're definitely listening. Good. Maybe they can help.

A moment later, Sophie says, "If we can do something to save this class, I'm in."

I look up. "Really?"

The bell rings. Ms. Harper calls from the stage, "See you tomorrow! Keep working on those lines!"

Grace rushes over and says, "I heard you talking about saving musical theater. Tell me everything."

I grin. She *was* listening. "I have an idea."

"As long as it's better than telling the principal that his plan is terrible," Grace says with an eye roll.

"Yeah, Grace already tried that," Jack says, his curls spilling across his forehead as he tucks his script into his backpack.

I turn back to Grace and say, "You d-did what?"

She beams. "I walked right up to Mr. Sinclair during lunch and I gave him a piece of my mind."

My mouth drops open. "Seriously?" I sling my bag over my shoulder as we move toward the exit.

"Oh yes, I did!"

"She definitely did," says Sophie. "It was awesome."

"How'd that work out?" I say. I wish I had the same lunch period as them.

Grace purses her lips. "He said he was sorry and told me to study more."

I groan. "That's not cool."

We walk quickly toward the double doors to the bus loading area.

"So what are we going to do about it?" Sophie says.

"We're going to write letters," I say.

Jack says, "That won't work! Mr. Sinclair will just throw them in the trash!"

I smile. "G-good thing we're not sending them to Mr. Sinclair, then."

Sophie leans closer, her lips curling into a smile around her braces.

"We're sending them to everyone else. His boss, his boss's boss, the newspaper, everyone! They're going to know what's going on and that we're not happy about it," I say.

Grace cheers and pumps her fist in the air. "YES! That could actually work." She shakes her head and says, "You are tiny but fierce."

I'm not tiny. She's just tall.

"GET TO YOUR BUSES," a teacher yells across the courtyard. "NOW!"

"Tomorrow morning before homeroom," Grace says. "Meet in the lobby. We're doing this."

I sprint to my bus, climb the stairs, and find packed seats everywhere except next to Ben and next to Maddie.

Ben scoots over so I can hurl myself into the seat. I take big gulps of air that taste like exhaust fumes, which makes me cough and sputter as the bus engine revs to life.

"Another close one," he says as the school gets smaller behind us. "Have you thought about running track?"

I cough-laugh. "If I were any good at running, I

wouldn't"—*cough*—"be cutting it so close." I peek over my left shoulder. Maddie sits slumped in the seat, and my heart breaks. I've never seen her look so sad. But she doesn't want me to sit with her. She told me so herself. I turn back around.

Ben flips open his notebook and starts sketching. "What were you doing, anyway?"

I shrug. "Just finishing up with musical theater."

"I didn't know you could sing." He looks up. "I'm the worst singer ever."

I wish he wouldn't put himself down like that. "Maybe you just haven't found the right song. Everyone can sing," I say, looking him in the eye the whole time. I promised Ms. G that I would try to make better eye contact when I'm talking—even if I stutter.

"Nope," he says with a shake of his head. He goes back to his drawing. "Not me. My dog howls when I sing."

I laugh. "No way."

"It's true." He chuckles. "I finally gave up because I didn't want to hurt her ears."

Maddie's voice cuts through the music. "Leave me alone!"

Ben and I immediately turn in our seats, just in time to see Tristan grab Maddie's notebook. The red one. The one she writes all her thoughts in and won't even let me see. Maddie grabs for it, and he tosses it to a girl across the aisle. She passes it to the person behind her. I want to rush down the aisle and help, but what can I do about it? I'd get in trouble for getting up. I sit up on my knees so I can follow the notebook.

The speaker crackles to life. The bus driver says, "I don't know what you're doing back there, but it needs to STOP. Now."

The notebook disappears into the back of the bus. I glance at Maddie, who's scanning the faces of kids behind her. She turns back around, her eyes full of panic. I wonder what she wrote in that notebook. I know what I write at home, and I'd never let anyone read it. Ever. I face the front and hug my legs to my chest, resting my head on my knees.

Ben glances at me. "It's just going to get worse. You know that, right?"

Yes, I know! I sigh. "Yeah, I kind of figured."

He lowers his voice. "It was really brave of her to snitch."

I snap my head up so fast, he jumps. "How do you know it was her?"

"I heard Tristan and Josh talking about it in the hallway."

"Yeah, but how do they know for sure?"

He glances back at their seat and says, "They saw her leave the principal's office on their way there."

"Everyone got called to the office that day."

"But they think she was the first one. I don't know."

We ride along in silence for a moment or two. I can't believe they talked about it where Ben could hear them. And now Ben thinks Maddie did a good thing. I wish I could tell him that I did, too. Maybe I didn't say it, which doesn't count as much, but at least I wrote it. I rest my head on my knees again.

Ben makes a few more loops on the page and holds it up. "Like it?"

It's like his other sketch where he's an alien and they're taking him to their ship, except this time he drew me standing next to him. I guess he thinks I'm an alien, too?

"It's really good," I say. I frown. "Hey, Ben?"

"Yeah?"

"There's just one problem."

"What?"

"We *do* belong here."

Mom and I have an early mother-daughter dinner because Dad had to stay late at work today for a meeting.

I wonder where Maddie's notebook is now. I roll my carrots around on the plate, separating them from the pile of peas.

"Charlotte."

"Hmm?"

"Give peas a chance."

I give Mom a half smile. Maddie's pages will be all over the school tomorrow. Oh no. They could be *online*. I didn't even think about that. If she ever needed a friend, it's right now.

Mom frowns. "Aren't you the least bit excited?"

"About what?"

She feels my forehead with her hand. "Are you sick?"

"No." But I feel like human garbage. Does that count?

"*Wicked*! It's tomorrow night!"

"OH! It is! I completely forgot!"

Mom shakes her head.

As soon as dinner's over, I call Maddie's cell. It goes straight to voice mail, which never happens. I frown and dial her parents' number. The phone rings twice, and her mom answers.

"Hi, um, is Maddie there?"

There's a pause. "Charlotte Andrews, is that you?" In the background, I hear Maddie say, "What! Charlotte?"

It's not too late. I can hang up the phone *right now* and pretend this never happened. But I won't, because I can't get Maddie's haunted, panicked eyes out of my mind. What was it Ms. Harper said? *Tell the truth. Make it count.* I brace myself. "Yes."

"Hey, hon." Maddie's mom clears her throat. "I heard you had a rough time."

I gulp. I wonder how much Maddie told her. "Yeah." I say. "It's, er, different now."

As if she just read my mind, Maddie's mom says, "Charlotte." I don't know how moms do it, but they can say my name and have it mean much more. It's just one word, but when she says it, it's like she's saying, *Sweetheart, I know there's more to it than that.* And then she actually says, "I know all about it."

My heart plummets through the floor. I knew it. "You d-d-do?"

"Of course I do. Maddie told me." Her voice is gentle. "She's been having a hard time, too. Why don't you sit with her again?"

I hug my knees to my chest and fight the tightening in my throat. I can't cry now. "I, um, I didn't know—that um, that is, what happened was—" The giant lump in my throat chokes my words, making them come out in a squeak.

The line is silent for a moment. This is going to be so much harder than I thought.

Finally her mom says, "Maddie doesn't understand, and I'm having a hard time with it myself. We miss you."

*And I miss you.* I'm so ashamed of what I've done. My lungs feel like they're getting smaller by the second. I can't breathe. I blurt out, "I have to go."

"Wait. Don't you want to talk to Maddie?"

I did. I do. I just can't even speak right now. The questions are too hard, and my answers too shameful. "I'm sorry. I need to g-g-go," I say, my voice cutting in and out.

"Wait a min—"

"Goodbye, sorry," I whisper, and click off the phone.

I sit down on my bed with the receiver in my hand. The tears roll down my cheeks. It's not like I didn't know this would happen, but . . . I'm so ashamed. How long will it be until her mom tells my mom? What if she calls her? My breath catches. My mom won't believe it, which will make it even worse. She sees me as someone who always does the kind thing, but I stopped being that person the moment I boarded the school bus. She has no idea who I really am.

I place the phone back on the base and burrow under the covers. Why couldn't I have held it together long enough to talk to Maddie? I needed to tell her that I'm still here. She has to know. I wipe my eyes on my sleeve. Just once, I wish I could do something right.

Ben said it was really brave of Maddie to speak up, and he's right. It must have taken so much courage to walk into Mr. Sinclair's office like that and tell him what happened. There's no way Ben would ever call me brave when I can't even apologize to Maddie.

The phone rings. I bolt up and wait for the caller ID to flash across the screen. My heart hammers in my chest. *Please don't be Maddie's mom. Please don't be Maddie's mom.* Every muscle tenses. My grandma's name and number appear, and the words "In Use" blink when someone answers. I breathe a huge sigh of relief as I sink back into my pillow.

What am I going to do when Maddie's mom *does* call? Or when my mom calls *her*?

I study the ceiling fan as it spins. What was I thinking? That everything would magically be okay if I called Maddie to say I'm sorry that she lost her notebook? I sigh. It wouldn't have helped her, but maybe I would've felt better.

I'm the worst.

## CHAPTER FOURTEEN

# SOMETHING WICKED

When I get on the bus the next morning, I'm ready. Anything could happen with Maddie's notebook pages. Someone could read them out loud and humiliate her. They could give everyone their own copy of her notebook. They could leave the pages all over the school. But so far, there's nothing weird, except Maddie isn't here. I don't think she's ever missed a day of school in her life. I study the kids around me, sprawling out of their cramped seats and into the aisle. No one looks like they're plotting some kind of disaster; they all look bored and tired. They had lots of energy when they wanted to throw around her notebook yesterday.

What will I do if Maddie's pages are put on display? Try

to reach out to her again? If it were my journal out there somewhere, I'd be puking right now. I pull out my notebook and stare at a blank page. There's so much cruelty everywhere. There doesn't have to be. Maybe, just maybe, I can do something to change that. All I have to do is reach a lot more kids with my notes.

I write:

It's okay if you're not perfect.

I wish I could be like you.

If you need a sign, this is it. Don't you dare give up!

I tear the messages off in strips, fold them into squares, and stick them into my pocket. Just like my other notes, I don't sign them with my real name. No one is going to care where they came from. It's the words that matter. I saw Ben after he read my note, and now I know what words can do. I just hope they find their way to kids who need them.

And then I realize that I know two kids who *really* need them. Tristan and Josh would never listen to me on the bus. But maybe, just maybe, a note would help. Ms. Harper wants me to write about something that's important to me. And this is *really* important.

Dear Tristan,

I stop. I started the other letters with something good about that person. What can I possibly say about Tristan? I don't know him at all, and what I do know isn't kind. I can't just write something that isn't true. He would know it wasn't real, and the whole point is to make it *mean* something. But then I think about the lunch line, and it comes to me.

> You are so strong. I'll bet no one knows you're having a hard time right now, but don't worry—I won't tell anyone. Middle school is hard for me, too. Sometimes I feel like I'm never going to be strong enough. Maybe you feel that way, too.

I search for the right words.

> But you can be kind. I think way deep down, you are. The strongest people are. Don't be afraid to show it.
> I hope things get better soon.

I read over the note and let my pen hover over the place for my signature. But it doesn't feel right anymore to sign it as "The Biggest Chicken at Carol Burnett Middle." A chicken wouldn't write this note. A chicken wouldn't do anything at all. I fold up the note and write Tristan's name on it. It's a letter from no one. It doesn't need a signature.

When I get to school, I quickly walk by the bathrooms, glance up and down the crowded hallway, and slide the note into the slats of Tristan's locker. I duck back to the bathroom just in time to pass Tristan in the middle of a group of kids. If I play this just right, maybe I can watch him read it! I bend down to pretend-tie my shoelaces by the wall while he approaches his locker.

He retrieves a book from his bag and stashes it in his locker, and then he pulls out my note.

A random kid grazes my shin with their shoe as they pass by me.

"Ow!" I say. I can't stay here; it's too dangerous. I stand up and shuffle over to wait my turn for the water fountain. I can see Tristan from the side as he unfolds the piece of paper. I bend down and press the lever, and the water goes straight up my nose. I have *no* future as a spy! I wipe my face and try again.

Tristan leans against the locker, head bent down. He's reading my note. The bag in his hand falls to the ground, forgotten.

"Hurry up!" some kid behind me says.

I step away from the water fountain and walk down the hallway. I sneak a glance at Tristan as I pass by just in time to see him frown and fold up the note. For a split second, I think he might crumple it into a ball like I did with Ms. Garrett's notes, but instead he slips it into his pocket and closes his locker.

I don't know if the note will help. But it feels good to try. I head down the hallway and find Grace and Sophie huddled over a cell phone.

"Hey!" I say. I drop my bag next to them. "What are you watching?"

"Shh!" Sophie hisses, but she angles her phone so I can see the screen.

"Turn it up," Grace says.

Maddie's face is on the screen, tears spilling down her cheeks. "You just don't know what it's like. You don't. You think it's so funny, that it's all a big joke, but I'm not laughing!"

I cover my mouth with my hand. Oh my gosh, what has she done? What have *I* done?

"Just stop. Please." Her lower lip trembles. "It's not supposed to be like this! I don't know when we all stopped being kind. I didn't do anything wrong. *They* did, and every day, the kids on my bus make my life awful." She wipes her eyes on her sleeve. "So anyway, I just wanted to say that if you feel alone out there, I get it." Her voice cracks. "I've never felt so alone in my whole life." The video ends. At the bottom, it says "4,000 views."

Grace shakes her head. "Wow."

"She's in my math class." Sophie turns off the screen. "Her name's Maddie."

My mouth goes dry. This is all because of the Bad Thing. It's my fault.

"Sounds like an awful bus," Grace says. "Where'd you find that, anyway?"

"Someone sent me the link. It's online," Sophie says. Her phone dings. And dings. And dings again. "Oh my gosh!" she says. "Stop!" She changes it to vibrate and drops it into her bag.

My stomach twists into a knot. I slide to the floor and hug my knees.

The buzzing continues from Sophie's bag.

"I feel so bad for that girl," Grace says.

This is why Maddie wasn't on the bus today. My lungs feel like they're shrinking. What happens now? I wish I could tell someone that I left her alone, that I'm part of the reason why she's so upset. But who would understand? *I* don't even understand, and I'm the one who did it. What will Tristan and Josh do when they find out she posted a video?

Jack approaches us. "Sorry. We got stuck in bus traffic." He taps his phone screen and holds it up for us. "Have you seen this?" Maddie's teary eyes stare back. I think they're going to follow me everywhere today, and maybe for the rest of my life. Why did I ever think it was okay to stop speaking up for her? To just not say anything at all?

Grace says, "Just watched it. Hey, send that to me, will you? I want to figure out who those kids are."

"Yeah, no kidding. They're the worst," Jack says, tapping out the message and putting away his phone.

"Totally," I say, looking from one to the other, with panic bubbling in my chest. What will they do if they find out it's me who made Maddie feel this bad? I may not be the one bullying her now. But what I did—the way I abandoned her—it's worse. They'll never talk to me again if they know what a bad friend I am.

Jack drops his bag at his feet. "So, did I miss anything else? Where are we sending the letters for musical theater, Charlotte?"

They all look at me. I ignore my pounding heart and make my mind switch from Maddie to musical theater.

I know this plan could work. I try to speak slowly so I won't stutter as much. "So, I was thinking we need to write to every single p-person on the school board. Then there's the superintendent. And we definitely need to send a letter to every newspaper we can find." I pull a piece of paper out of my notebook. "I made a list."

Jack reaches for it. "Can we split them up?"

"Actually," I say, "I was thinking we should *all* write letters to each person. More letters means it's a bigger deal." At least, I hope it does.

Grace says, "Ooh, I like that. More noise means more attention."

"Exactly. They're not going to be able to ignore us. And we need to invite them to the play. If they can just *see* what we can do, maybe they'll change their minds." I look up to find them all nodding in agreement.

"Great idea! Shouldn't we get more people to write letters with us, then?" Sophie asks. "We should talk to other people in class."

Wow. If everyone else sends letters, we might actually be able to do something. And all because I said something about it to Sophie in class. I nod. "That's a great idea. T-t—" I pause and take a deep breath like I practiced with Ms. G and look each of them in the eye. "Tell everyone."

They head toward their homerooms, and I start toward mine. I can't stop thinking about writing letters. What if I wrote a note for Josh, too? He seemed upset that he had to work on football all the time for his dad. Maybe some encouragement would help him—and help Maddie. I sneak another piece of paper under my notebook during attendance.

*Dear Josh,*

*You inspire me because you always work so hard, even when you must be exhausted from football and homework. I know it's not easy. I think that's pretty amazing.*

I fold up the note, write his name on it, and on my way to class, I stick it into his locker. I hope it makes him feel better. Maybe if he gets a kind note, he'll be inspired to be kinder.

I also stick each of the folded notes I wrote on the bus into random lockers.

I'm not going to be quiet anymore.

"Enjoy the show," an usher says as she hands me a Playbill for *Wicked*. "Your seats are down the center, to the right." The theater's lobby is draped in burgundy and gold, with tinkly glass chandeliers and portraits of old people.

I squeeze my mom's arm and try not to squeal as we walk down the aisle. It looks like it's a sold-out show! We settle into red velvet seats that are a million times more comfortable than the plastic ones in our school auditorium. When I lean forward to check out everything, I spot Aubrey a few rows ahead, waving at someone in the balcony. What are the odds of her being at the same show? I'll bet there are more musical theater kids here, especially since the show is only being performed a few times.

"Hey, Mom?"

"Yes, Charlotte?"

I grin up at her. "This is really great. Thank you!"

She gives me a side hug. "Happy early birthday, kiddo."

When the lights go down and the first bars of music play, my smile gets bigger.

And the musical is so much like school. Enemies become friends, friends become enemies, and it doesn't always make sense. I can't help but think of Maddie and my mountain of guilt, but I try to put it out of my mind. This is for my birthday, and tonight is supposed to be fun.

When the house lights go up for intermission, Mom beams at me. "Do you like it so far?"

"What's not to like? This is awesome."

"I think we're going to need some popcorn," Mom says.

"Sounds good," I say.

We head to one of the concession lines in the lobby, breathing in the smell of coffee and buttered popcorn. I catch a glimpse of someone who looks a lot like Maddie disappearing into the restroom. "Hey, Mom? I'm going to run to the bathroom, okay?"

"Sure," she says. "I'll watch for you."

I dart into the restroom. "Maddie?" I check under the

stalls, looking for shoes I recognize. "Maddie, are you in here?"

I guess it wasn't her. I step out into the hallway as the lights flicker.

Mom rushes over to me with a bucket of popcorn and two Cherry Cokes. "Better hurry! It's about to start!"

We're just finding our seats again when Glinda walks out onstage with a microphone, followed by the Wicked Witch. "Ladies and gentlemen, we have a very special guest in the audience with us tonight. And before we resume the show, we want to introduce her to you. Maddie Hobson, will you please come to the stage?"

I gasp. It *was* her!

Maddie stands up in the front row—how did she get those seats?—and runs around to the side of the stage. The two actresses take turns hugging her. The one playing the Wicked Witch puts her arm around Maddie's shoulders and turns back to the audience. "Maddie has been having a hard time at school, and she posted an emotional video about it last night. What she didn't know is that it would go viral today, and that we would see it before the show. We can't take back all the hurt this young lady has been through, but we *would* like your help reminding her that there is goodness in the world. If you support Maddie and want her to know you're rooting for her, let's give her a big round of applause!"

The auditorium goes wild. I clap once or twice in between stealing glances up at my mom. She looks at me like she doesn't even know me. I'm so dead.

"We wish you all the best, Maddie."

Maddie hugs the Wicked Witch.

Glinda says, "There's just *one* more thing." She goes off-curtain and returns with a bouquet of red roses and a big envelope. "From all of us in Oz, we hope to see you again this summer . . . ON BROADWAY!"

"What!" Maddie squeals.

My jaw drops.

"That's right! We're sending you and your mom to New York. You'll have backstage passes and everything. Let's give her another hand, folks!"

The cheers are deafening.

Maddie wipes her face and gives Glinda a huge hug. She disappears off the stage with her roses and her card.

My mom's eyes bore holes into the side of my face. I stare down at my feet.

"You and I need to talk."

I nod and dig my toe into the floor. *So* dead.

The lights go back down, and the play continues. *Wicked* shows the other side of the story between the Wicked Witch and Glinda, and all the moments of hurt and love that make friendship so complicated. But nothing lasts forever, and before I know it, the show ends, and real life is waiting.

At first, I think we're going to have to face Maddie and her mother, but Mom makes a beeline for one of the side doors. Once we're safely in the SUV and the doors are locked, she pulls out her phone.

I'm going to be sick.

A moment later, Maddie's video plays. I listen, feeling an inch smaller with each passing second. When Maddie says, "I've never felt so alone in my whole life," I cringe and glance over at Mom. She looks the saddest I've ever seen her. She shakes her head, and when she looks at me, her eyes are glassy. "I knew something was wrong." She sighs. "Tell me, Charlotte. It doesn't matter how bad it is. It's time."

I feel a catch in my throat, and the tension moves up my jaw. "I don't know." My face grows hot, and my eyes start to fill with tears.

"You used to tell me everything." She starts the car and pulls out into traffic. "Middle school doesn't mean you have to do everything by yourself, you know. I'm still your mom." She glances over at me. "I will *always* be your mom, and I'm going to love you no matter what. And this has been going on for *weeks*. Aren't you tired of keeping it all bottled up inside?"

I stare down at my hands. It's like she's in my head.

"Tell me."

At first I say a word or two, and then a few "I don't knows." But the story wants to be told, and I've been carrying it on my own for so long. I start with Ben and the gum, and how I, Charlotte Andrews, did the right thing, and it didn't matter. When I get to the part where they called me ugly and made fun of my speech, steam practically comes out of her nose.

"You wait until I speak with Mr. Sinclair tomorrow."

"No!" I cry, my voice growing louder. "You c-can't!"

"I'm your mom. I sure can."

The tears start coming again. "Look, I know you don't understand, but you *can't* do that. You can't! If you do, sure, it will be fine for a day or two, but then T-Tristan and Josh will be worse than they were when it happened. The only way I get to survive is if we don't say anything. If you do, my life is *over*!"

In a quiet voice, she says, "What happened next?"

I squeeze my eyes shut and tell her every detail about the Bad Thing, how that moment passed by so fast and I walked by Maddie on the bus like she was nothing.

Mom listens, the crease between her eyebrows deepening.

"And then it was too late to fix it. I wanted to, but . . . I made a mess of everything." I hang my head and sob, tears dripping onto my glasses, until I feel the warmth of her hand on my shoulder.

"Oh, Charlotte."

I look up at her in between ragged breaths. We're in our driveway, and I didn't even notice.

She wipes a tear from my cheek. "I wish you'd told me sooner."

I take off my fogged-up glasses. "But I couldn't! You would've told Mr. Sinclair, and then it would've been so much worse. You should've heard the guys bragging about getting away with everything. I never wanted to leave her sitting by herself. But after all that happened, I just couldn't do it again. That day was so awful. You just can't imagine what it was like."

She unbuckles her seat belt and wraps both arms around me. "No, I can't. But I know someone who can."

I sob into her shoulder. *Maddie, Maddie, Maddie.*

She sighs. "So, you left the only friend you had to avoid getting picked on."

My eyes well up with more tears. "Yeah." It sounds even worse when she says it out loud. Maybe there will be a day when I won't feel guilty and afraid, but I can't picture what that would even feel like. Is that my punishment for this? To feel this way forever?

Mom rummages in the glove compartment and hands me a few fast-food napkins. "You're in a pickle, kiddo."

"I d-d"—I want to say "don't know how to fix it," but I

can't get past the *D* sound. I pause and take a deep breath. "How can I fix it?"

"You can't fix this. But you can start by saying you're sorry."

"Mom! I already tried talking to her at school. I called her. I even wrote her a note saying I was sorry, but she crumpled it up and left it in my seat! She's not going to listen to me." I blow my nose into a napkin.

"That doesn't matter. You say it anyway, even if nothing changes. 'Sorry' is for you as much as it is for her." Her eyes soften. "I know this is hard. I'll help you find the right words."

I rest my face in my hands and let my hair spill over my fingers. It all seems so pointless now. "She told me I can't sit with her, Mom."

"Can you blame her? She's just hurt. She didn't mean it."

"I called her again yesterday."

"And?"

"Her mom answered." I sniffle. "She started saying all these things, and I just couldn't do it. I told her I had to go."

She sighs. "That bad, huh?"

I blow my nose with a loud honk. "It was brutal."

"You can always try again." She hands me another napkin.

My eyes widen. "Not with her mom, I can't!" The shame was too much the last time. I'm *supposed* to be Maddie's friend. How can I talk to her mom again when she knows what I've done?

Mom considers me a moment. "You know, choosing not to make a choice is still a choice. You have to *do something.*"

I nod. I figured that much out all by myself.

And as she cuts off the engine, I read the pause she takes before she opens the door. It means: *Do the right thing, Charlotte.*

## CHAPTER FIFTEEN

# TIMING

When I get on the bus the next morning, Maddie looks me right in the eye. She knew I was at the play last night. I'd only been talking about it forever. She knows my mom knows.

I slow down and try to smile as I approach her seat, but she turns and looks out the window.

I slide into a seat in the back, pull out my notebook, and do the only thing I *can* do. I write more notes:

The world is better because you're in it.

Don't underestimate yourself.

*You inspire me.*

*You don't have to be afraid.*

*You are loved.*

I fold and pocket the notes and look up when laughter rings out. Tristan and Josh waltz down the aisle, doing fake bows as they pass Maddie and slide into the seat behind her. For the first time ever, there's a seventh-grade girl sitting next to her.

I look away and make eye contact with Lyric. She says, "Did you see the video?"

I nod.

She starts to say something else and then stops.

Weird. Why is she talking to me?

When we exit the bus, Mr. Sinclair stands at the back door of the school, his mouth set in a straight line. He motions for Maddie, and they walk ahead. I'm close enough that I see the crowd part when they enter the lobby. There's almost a hush that falls over the hall, and a moment later, they disappear through the glass doors into the office.

I make my way to homeroom, stopping along the way to leave my notes on a bench, in a locker, and on the bathroom sink. I hope they help someone. Someone like Maddie.

As I enter the classroom behind two guys, one says, "Did you know Maddie's going on tour with a rock star?"

The other replies, "No way! I heard some celebrity called and asked her to the spring dance."

"Nice!"

"Where d-did you hear that?" I ask.

He rolls his eyes. "It's all over the news. Duh. Where have you been?"

I sling my bag down at my desk. *Have I lost Maddie forever? Is she going to make all new friends now?* It might really be too late for me to make things right. But it isn't too late for musical theater. I have a voice. It's time I use it, just like Mom said I should. I pull out my notebook and write:

Dear Newspaper Editor,

My name is Charlotte Andrews, and I am in sixth grade at Carol Burnett Middle. I'm going to be in a musical this year for the first time in my whole life. It also might be the last time because they're taking away musical theater next year! They say it's so we can have a reading enrichment program, and a bunch of the teachers have to teach it. But we already read in our other classes. And we read in musical theater—how do you think we memorize our lines?

Please help tell our story so that maybe, just maybe, whoever's in charge will change their minds. I know I'm just a kid, but I hope you believe me when I tell you that we need this class. We don't take big tests in musical theater, so no one thinks it's important. There's just us, a stage, and all the work we do in between the beginning and opening night. But we put our whole hearts into it. The only way you'll understand is if you come and see for yourself. We're performing The Wizard of Oz in two weeks, October 18–20. Hope to see you there.

Yours truly,
Charlotte Andrews

The bell rings. I fold the letter and put it into my binder. It feels so small compared to everything else, but it's a start.

I stand shyly in the doorway of Ms. G's office with my gym bag slung over my shoulder.

"Hey, Charlotte!" Ms. G says, glancing up from her desk.

"Hey."

"I hope you're not too upset with me for taking you out of PE." She winks.

I manage a half smile. "I guess I'll live. I was really looking forward to smelling like dirty socks for the rest of the day, but you've ruined everything."

She chuckles. "You can go back if you want, and I can meet up with you later!"

"N-no, no. That's okay."

"How's everything?"

I shrug and take my usual seat across from her desk. "Oh! I got to see *Wicked* last night!"

"Lucky! I've wanted to see that for years now. Someday!"

"Yeah, it was awesome." Except for the part where my mom found out who I really am, and I lay in bed last night wondering if she still likes me. I know she loves me, but does she *like* me? Sometimes I don't like myself because of what I've done. How can other people like me if I don't like myself?

"How's *your* play going?"

I perk up just thinking about it. "It's good! You should hear the music."

"I think I just might have to do that."

I push my glasses up on my nose and grin.

"Okay, let's get serious for a second," Ms. G says now. "How are you doing with your goals?"

"Fine." Everything is fine, fine, fine.

"So, when you start to stutter, what do you do?" She sips her coffee.

"I've been trying to pause. Then I take a deep breath and say the word again. Sometimes I say something completely different because I know the word is going to get stuck. Sometimes I say it anyway."

"That's good. When would you say you stutter the most?"

The words just fall out of my mouth. "When everyone's looking at me, or when my mouth can't keep up with my brain. It also happens more when I get excited or nervous. And sometimes for no reason at all."

She raises an eyebrow. "How's that working out for you onstage?"

"Better. I know what I'm going to say, and I just keep using easy onset. It's also easier to say the words when I'm playing someone else. I have no idea why, except that I'm not me anymore."

She smiles at me. "You know, there are some famous actors who stutter."

"Really?" I can't even imagine it.

"Really."

"But . . . how do they not get stuck on their lines?"

"I think they work with the script, and they keep trying. Just like you!"

I consider it for a moment. "It's just so weird that I'm

doing something that usually makes me stutter more. But it's not like it was my idea. My parents *made* me."

She laughs. "So I've heard."

I gasp. "They *told* you?"

"Sure did," she says. "Do you feel like being in musical theater is helping?"

I think for a moment. "I don't think I'll ever stop stuttering. But . . ." I search for the right words. "I'm not as afraid of messing up as I used to be."

She smiles. "I think that's great, Charlotte. Practicing onstage is making you more confident! Would you say you're doing better at looking people in the eye when you're talking to them?"

I nod. "Yeah, but you can't tell my mom! She'll say 'I told you so' for the rest of my life!"

Ms. G chuckles and rests her chin on her hand. "Okay," she muses. "I won't tell her, but don't you think it's kind of obvious?"

"No, I'm not *that* confident."

She says, "I was thinking *brave.*"

## CHAPTER SIXTEEN

# STAGING

The best part about being a tree and a horse is that I don't have to dance, which is probably the greatest casting decision ever. Instead I get to sit in the audience with Sophie and watch everyone else stage the songs. Ms. Harper reminded us *again* at the beginning of class that this is the last year that we get to do this. It won't be, if the other kids and I have anything to do with it!

Sophie passes me a note.

*Write any letters?*

I nod and flip open my notebook to show her.

After she reads it, she scribbles:

*This is really good! Can we share it? So the others can see an example?*

I nod.

She glances around quickly, and when she's sure no teachers are watching, she snaps a picture of it with her cell and sends out a group message to the theater kids with phones. Then she jots down.

*I wrote a letter to two school board members.*
*Mailed them today.*

The bell rings. Jack and Grace hop down from the stage and rush over to get their bags.

Sophie says, "But if we really want people to notice, we need more letters."

Jack says, "Hey, what are you doing this weekend?" as we push through the auditorium doors on our way to the buses.

I do a double take. Is he talking to me or Grace?

Grace shrugs. "No plans yet."

"Charlotte?" he says.

He's talking to *me*? "Uh, same."

"We should invite the rest of the class over to my dad's house to write letters. He won't care," Jack says.

Sophie grins. "Love it! What do you think, Charlotte?"

I nod. "Go big or go home!"

Jack clasps his hands together. "This is going to be awesome. I'll spread the word."

We split up and rush to our buses.

Once I'm seated, I pull out my notebook to work on another letter. After a few minutes, I realize we haven't left school yet. I tilt my head and look out the window to try to catch a glimpse of whatever is keeping us. Everything looks the same as it usually does. Then I hear a familiar voice and look up. Mr. Sinclair stands at the front of the bus, the PA mic in his hand. "Good afternoon, all. I just wanted to tell you that I have been investigating some news around this bus today, and I'm still not done."

Is it because of Maddie's video?

"If I hear any reports of bad behavior, if you so much as look at someone else unkindly, there will be severe consequences." He studies each seat. "And I might remind you of our school's policy on bullying. It won't be tolerated. Also, for those of you who participate in athletics and clubs, remember that they are a *privilege*. If you can't treat others with kindness, you will find yourselves ineligible to participate."

Josh and Tristan share a silent look of panic. Maddie didn't even mention them in the video, but the idea of losing their spots on the football team gets their attention.

"Do you see this camera?" He motions to a new lens above the bus driver's head. "It's going to be recording *everything* that happens on this bus. I expect there will be no more issues."

Finally Mr. Sinclair leaves, and the bus pulls away from the curb. I settle back into my seat and stare at the houses and the autumn leaves as we speed by. It's quieter than usual, but I can still hear kids talking about Maddie visiting movie stars and NFL teams. Maddie laughs with a girl sitting next to her, and it's like they're the best of friends. She never even talked to Maddie before today. Why would she start now? And why would that seventh grader sit with her this morning? I frown. They're being *too* nice.

## CHAPTER SEVENTEEN

# FAME

"**H**ave you talked to Maddie yet?" Mom asks as we all clean up the kitchen after dinner. It's our usual assembly line: Mom washes the pans, Dad dries them, and I put them away.

"No."

She frowns. "Why not?"

"I just . . . I don't know what to say. It's all going to come out wrong, and then I'll just make it worse."

Mom and Dad exchange glances. Mom hands him the last pan and dries her hands on a dishtowel. Without a word, she opens the kitchen junk drawer and rummages through it. Seconds later, she hands me some paper and a pen. "Then why don't you write her a letter? If you can't say the words, put them on paper."

"Mom! I already t-tried that, remember? She crumpled it up and left it on my seat."

"Then you try again. I'll help you." She sits down at the kitchen table and pats the seat next to her.

I drop down into the chair with a sigh and pick up the pen. It probably won't do any good, but I write,

Dear Maddie,

I stare at the words while I tap a drumbeat on the table.

Mom leans over. "What do you wish you could say to her right now?"

I lean over the paper and write:

I'm sorry.

"And?"

I shouldn't have stopped sitting with you. It was all because of Tristan and Josh. I made a mis—

She clears her throat. "I know they're part of the story, but Charlotte . . ." Her voice is gentle. "You need to take responsibility for what *you* did. Don't blame someone else, or your apology won't mean anything."

Tristan and Josh started it, yeah. But I made the choice that got us here. I broke my friendship with Maddie by leaving her to face the bullies alone. I return to the letter.

> ~~It was all because of Tristan and Josh.~~ I made a mistake. I knew it the second it happened, but it was too late. I couldn't take it back.

I click the end of my pen over and over again, making the ballpoint disappear and reappear. If only I could find the magic words to somehow make things right again. "I don't know what else to write."

Mom leans over the letter. "Let's see. . . . Apology, check. You told her you made a mistake. Check." She rests her chin on her hand. "Isn't there something you need to ask Maddie?"

I shrug. "I don't know."

"Oh yes, you do," Mom says with a pointed look.

She's right. I do know. But that doesn't make it any less difficult to ask. I write.

> Do you think you could ever forgive me?

"There ya go," Mom says. She gives my arm a reassuring pat. "Anything else you want to add?"

I shake my head.

"Then you're ready to sign it."

My hand wavers just a bit as I write:

Your friend, Charlotte

Maybe I can still be her friend. Maybe there's still time.

Mom smiles and hands me an envelope and a stamp. "You're all set. Put it in the mailbox tomorrow."

I look down at the letter and frown. I'm glad I wrote it, but it feels like it's too late. "What if Maddie thinks I'm just trying to be her friend because of all the attention she's g-g—" I pause and take a breath. It helps when I exhale as I say the word I'm having trouble saying. "Getting from famous people?"

Mom's smile fades. "She might. You can't control how people see things, Charlotte. All you can do is say you're sorry and hope she knows how much you care about her. That's it." As she stands to leave the table, she leans over and drops a kiss onto my head.

"What was that for?"

"For being you."

I look down. "I don't know how that's a good thing."

"Don't you talk about my daughter like that." She wraps her arms around me. "It's hard to admit when you're wrong.

It takes a lot of courage to do something about your mistakes."

I sigh. "It's still not the same as saying 'sorry' out loud." If I were really brave, I'd walk right up to Maddie in front of everyone and apologize. I know it. My mom knows it. Maddie knows it.

"This is how you get there," she says. "One step at a time. You'll see."

I give her a tight smile and go up to my bedroom. I hope she's right. I've felt helpless about Maddie for so long, and now part of me thinks that maybe this could fix things. This note is better than my last one. "I'm sorry" doesn't really mean much until you put more words and real feeling with your apology.

The right words really are powerful. I glance at my script for *The Wizard of Oz* on my dresser. What if my letters to save musical theater class could be just as powerful? I pick up my pencil. Before I know it, I've written three more letters, and my wrist hurts from writing so much. But I don't stop there. After I write lots of random notes of kindness for kids and stuff them into my bag, I crawl into bed. In the moment before I drift off to sleep, I ask myself, *Have I done enough?*

The next morning, I stick four letters into our mailbox on my way to the bus stop. One for Maddie and three to save musical theater class. The notes for other kids are folded in my pockets and in my backpack.

I reach the bus stop and drop my backpack to the sidewalk.

Lyric puts away the phone she begged for the whole time she was in fifth grade. I'm guessing it was her birthday present last year, but I don't know for sure.

"Why'd you stop sitting with Maddie?" Lyric asks.

I stare at her. Last year Lyric's birthday party balloons appeared on their mailbox, same as always. I watched the older kids arrive for twenty minutes that Saturday. My mom said maybe my invitation had gotten lost in the mail and they'd give us a call when I didn't show up, but I knew the truth. I wasn't invited. Until then, I'd hoped we'd be friends again. But it never happened. And now she wants to ask me about Maddie?

I shrug. "Just wanted to sit in the back, I guess."

It's like she's looking straight through me. "Okay. . . . So, are you still friends?"

Where is this coming from? Why does she even care? "Uh, yeah, I guess so." I don't know what else to say.

"Could you ask her if she'll introduce me to the band from that new superhero movie?" she blurts out.

I raise my eyebrows. Is she serious? "She doesn't know them."

"Does so." She takes out her phone and scrolls through Twitter. "See?" she says when she finds the right tweet.

I guess she does know them. "I can't ask her to introduce you. It would be weird."

The bus whines its way up the hill and turns down our street.

She purses her lips. "I knew you weren't friends anymore. Or you'd be sitting with her."

My face grows hot. "We are," I say, humiliation bubbling up in me. "B-b—" I pause. *Slow down, Charlotte!* "Uh, but you and I aren't. You can't just t-talk to me when you want something."

Lyric's jaw drops.

For just a split second, I feel a twinge of guilt, but it passes. I'm still angry about the way she treated me. "If you want to meet the band, ask her yourself." It was weird when the older girls on the bus started sitting with Maddie, but now Lyric is asking for favors? It all makes sense. They just want to use Maddie. The thought makes me furious. Maddie is a *person,* and a really good one we used to be lucky enough to know.

I freeze. *We* used to be that lucky. Lyric and me. But Lyric made a choice last year when she dropped both Maddie and me as friends, and then . . . I did the same thing to Maddie! I'm just like Lyric.

The bus stops at the driveway and the door opens.

I can't let Lyric hurt Maddie again by asking for favors after all this time. Maddie would know Lyric was just trying to use her. I glance over my shoulder on the first step and say, "Hey—don't ask her to introduce you." I look her right in the eye. "Everyone wants something from her now. She doesn't know who her real friends are anymore." I cringe inside on the last sentence. Am I a real friend?

Lyric frowns and follows behind me. "I, uh, didn't think about that."

"Yeah." I walk down the aisle, and Maddie's there. Her braid is super neat for a change, and . . . is she wearing makeup? She makes eye contact with me for a moment and turns to an eighth-grade girl who's never spoken to her before now.

Does this mean what I think it means? Josh and Tristan aren't on the bus yet, but if people start sitting with Maddie, will the boys stop bullying her? I'd give anything to sit next to Maddie. But I can't do that because she won't let me. Not unless she reads my letter and forgives me.

But I can sit in the seat behind her so Josh and Tristan can't. At least that's doing *something*. I drop into the seat and put a neatly folded note with the words You're stronger than you know next to me.

If someone new rode our bus this morning, they'd have no idea that anything horrible had ever happened. The most popular kids gather around Maddie. They offer her candy, play with her hair, and ask her when the pro wrestlers are coming to PE. It's like that moment in *Rudolph the Red-Nosed Reindeer* when his nose saves the day and just like that, BOOM. He's in the club. All the other reindeer decide he's awesome and let him hang out after making fun of him for so long.

Maddie glances at me over her seat and frowns.

My stomach drops. My timing is all wrong. She probably thinks I'm sitting here because of all the celebrities. But I just want my best friend back. Maybe we can pick up where we left off?

*No, we can't.*

Ms. Harper starts English class with a piece of paper in her hand at the front of the room. "Before we get started writing today, I wanted to take a minute to share this with you. There's been so much good writing in here. I've seen everything from comics to mysteries, and you're all keeping me turning pages to find out what happens next! The other day, one of you wrote a powerful essay that I just have to share with the class." She clears her throat and begins to read. I sit straight up in my seat at the sound of a few familiar lines. She says, " 'If you don't speak up, no one will ever hear your voice. And you *have* a voice!' " That's *my* essay! It sounds different from when I wrote it in my head. The words are stronger when Ms. Harper says them.

I feel a flush of heat rise up my neck and into my face. I've never been anything close to extraordinary, and now a teacher is saying my words are *powerful*? No one has ever read my work to the class before. I glance around at the other kids listening to my words.

Ms. Harper finishes the last line and looks up and beams. "This person really grasped the assignment. Keep up the good work, folks. Now let's log some words!" She places the paper on her desk and settles down to write.

I lean back in my seat. Am I dreaming? I must be dreaming. I glance up at Ms. Harper, who, at the exact same time, looks up at me. She winks and goes back to her paper.

My face might split in two, I'm smiling so hard. She liked my work! I glance down at my blank sheet of paper and feel a small swell of panic. What do I write? If she liked my essay on speaking up, she probably wants something else that's real. I can't disappoint Ms. Harper, but it's not like I can tell her about Maddie and the bus. I have other stuff I can write about, though. After talking to Lyric this morning, there's so much in my head that I think it will explode if I don't write down some of it. I can be careful. I'll write in code, and she'll never know I'm talking about Maddie! I write about kid celebrities, and how so many people must be super nice to them just because they're *them*. And that it must be terrible to never know who your real friends are, and who's just trying to use you.

I rest my chin on my hand. I still can't believe that Tristan and Josh actually left Maddie alone this morning. They sat a few seats back and acted like she wasn't even there, like they hadn't just spent the last few weeks making her life miserable. They're not pretending to be her friends. *Yet.*

I write, It's not real. They just want to say they know you. But what happens when no one cares anymore, and you're just someone who was cool for five minutes?

It didn't take much convincing to talk my mom into driving me to Jack's dad's house. Word of our letter-writing party spread quickly among the theater parents. Mom said, "What did I tell you? I *knew* you'd make friends in musical theater!" She was so excited that I would be hanging out with other kids, I'm surprised she didn't leave tire marks in front of his driveway. Only one thing held her back. As I stepped out of the car, she said, "Wouldn't it be nice if you called Maddie and asked her over for tomorrow?"

"Um, I g-guess?" I offered. "But, Mom, I can't."

"Sure you can," she said, nodding with encouragement. Then she left me with a bowl of bean dip and a promise that she'd be back in two hours.

Before I can ring the bell, the door opens, and Jack's dad whisks me inside. In the kitchen, kids from class stand around, snacking on cookies, potato chips, and vegetables. There's a sweating ice bucket full of canned soft drinks at the end of the counter.

Sophie, Grace, and Jack sit at the table with a stack of paper and envelopes, and a growing pile of finished letters in the center. "Hey, Charlotte!" Jack says. "Is that bean dip?"

The doorbell rings, and Jack's dad darts into the hallway. I tug at my sweater, which is all of a sudden itchy and hot.

"Yeah." I set it on the table. Then I grab a drink, sit down, and pick up a piece of paper.

Aubrey strolls into the kitchen. "Hey, y'all!" she says, plopping down at the table with us.

The group chatters a few hellos.

Grace grins. "I'm loving your letter, Charlotte. It helped me a ton."

"Thanks."

"What letter?" Aubrey says.

Sophie hands her a copy of it. "I thought it was awesome and asked if we could share as a good example."

"'Awesome' is right," Jack says, holding out his fist. "Fist bump!"

I bump my hand into his, and he makes a "Boom" sound effect at the moment our knuckles touch.

Aubrey nods. "Oh yeah. I remember." She folds up my letter, puts it into her pocket, and picks up a blank piece of paper.

"My favorite part," Grace says, "is when you say"—she clears her throat—"'But we put our whole hearts into it. The only way you'll understand is if you come and see for yourself.'" She shakes her head. "That's so great. How did you come up with it?"

I shrug. "I don't know. It just— It's true. We *do* put our whole hearts into it." I reach for some chips. "And they don't understand, or they wouldn't be canceling musical theater."

"It's all about test scores," Grace says. "It has to be."

We all groan.

"How do you know?" Aubrey asks.

"My cousin said they did the same thing at her school. If scores aren't at the top, bye-bye, art classes. I even called her to make sure."

The pile of letters in the center of the table appears much smaller after that. We need to write more, and *fast*.

Aubrey dangles a finished letter in front of us. "Pass the stamps, please."

Jack pushes the roll of stamps across the table.

One of the kids at the counter comes over for another sheet of paper and hums the first line of a song from the radio. Jack joins in, and in two seconds flat, we're all singing. I glance up from my letter and take it all in. It reminds me of what I imagined my dream middle school would be like all those weeks ago. I return to my letter with a smile. If I doubted it before, I don't anymore. I belong here.

## CHAPTER EIGHTEEN

# I'M A WHAT?

Today it's *finally* time to do fittings for our costumes. We line up at the door to the wardrobe closet backstage in the auditorium. It's next to the dressing rooms, so that's convenient. The inside of it looks like a flea market exploded. There are suitcases, hats, scarves, and feather boas. Motorcycle jackets and taffeta. An entire wall of shoes. Ms. Harper and Ms. Bishop pace around the small space, calling out students' names and plucking hangers off racks. They wanted to buy some new costumes for the show, but the budget was cut. Ms. Harper said they had to "get creative" with their wardrobe closet. I'm afraid to see what I'll be wearing.

"Jack!" Ms. Harper calls.

Jack steps up.

She hands him a stack of silver clothing.

Jack holds it up, frowning. "Where's the hat?"

Ms. Harper smiles. "We'll add that once you're wearing the costume."

He disappears into the boys' dressing room.

Ms. Harper looks at her clipboard. "Grace! Come on down!" She disappears and returns with a blue gingham dress and slippers.

Grace says, "Now, that's what I'm talking about. Look at those shoes!"

"Go on, hurry."

"I'm going, I'm going," Grace says. She moves off to the girls' dressing room.

"Aubrey!" A big ball of poufy pink appears, and somewhere behind it, Ms. Bishop.

Aubrey takes the dress and holds it up to her shoulders. "Oh my gosh, it's *gor-geous!*"

I smile. It really is.

"Charlotte!" Ms. Harper beckons for me to approach.

She hands over a floor-length brown dress with long sleeves.

"This is a tree?"

"It will be," says Ms. Harper. "Sophie! Where's Sophie?"

I turn to go to the dressing room. It could still be okay. The material feels soft, so at least it's not going to be itchy.

Right inside the dressing room door, there's a long

counter with stools where some girls are already changing into Munchkin costumes. Mirrors line the space above the counter, and just above the mirrors is a long row of light-bulbs that illuminate the room in a warm glow. To the right, there's a table, a few cubbies, and a costume rack. Just past the corner of the cubbies, the room flows into a wider space with benches and racks to hang clothes on, and the entire wall is a mirror, like the kind in a dance studio. On the op-posite wall is a row of lockers. But the coolest thing is that there's a star on each one. I smile. I've always wanted my own star.

Grace says, "Hey, Charlotte! What do you think? Isn't it awesome?" She holds her arms out wide and poses in her Dorothy dress.

I almost gasp. The blue pops against her tawny brown skin, and the sequins on the slippers sparkle. "It's too per-fect. You look amazing."

"Thanks! Gotta go show Ms. Harper!"

I take my dress off the hanger and examine it closely. It's like crushed velvet, and there are these long things hanging from the arms. Hmm. I slip out of my jeans and shirt and pull the dress over my head. It goes all the way past my shoes and down to the floor. I could wear slippers under it, and no one would ever know! What in the world is this? I hold my arms straight out to my sides, like I would if I were doing jumping jacks. There's this lighter brown netting hanging down under each arm, like the connective tissue on a bat's wing. The sleeves go way past my arms, like some kind of wizard's robe. There's even a brown hood. I pull it up over my head and see only my face peeking out of the opening, my cheeks slightly flushed. I look like a bat-wizard. I definitely don't look like a tree.

I sigh and walk back to the wardrobe closet and Ms. Harper. Most of the kids have already changed or are still in the fitting rooms. Aubrey sizes me up in my bat-wizard nonsense and gives me a spectacular eye roll.

Ms. Harper says, "You're good to go, Jack!" He turns around, and I'm struck by how much taller he looks—and it's not just the upside-down funnel on his head, either. He's wearing a long-sleeved silver shirt and, over it, what looks like silver medieval armor. On his shoulders, there are shoulder pads that look like they were part of a football uniform and someone painted them metallic silver. His pants look like shiny silver sweatpants.

He half cringes when he sees my costume, and tries to cover by fist-bumping me as he passes by. Too late! I know I look ridiculous.

I step up to the doorway. "Ms. Harper."

She turns around. "Oh, wow! Look at you!"

"I don't look like a tree."

"Of course you don't!" She turns and goes to a box in the corner. "You don't have"—she turns back around—"THIS!"

Oh. My. Gosh. It looks like she's holding a fake potted plant that's been loaded down with apple ornaments. Before I can say a word, she plops it down onto my head.

"PERFECT!" she says.

I object.

"Take a look!"

I glance over at the long mirror on the wall, and it's as bad as I thought. It looks like one of my mom's hanging plants exploded on my head. I'm still stunned when Sophie approaches in her brown bat-wizard robe. Ms. Harper plunks a plant thing onto her head, too, approves, and says, "Thank you, ladies. The apple trees are ready for Oz!"

We hand over our houseplant hats and turn to leave.

"Hang on!" Ms. Harper calls after us.

I look over my shoulder.

"You still have to try on your horse costume!"

Sophie and I exchange glances while she goes to one of the tables and returns with two huge stacks of purple fabric.

She gives Sophie a stack, along with a huge horse head with bulging eyes. Then she hands me a smaller stack.

"You forgot the head," I say.

"No, I didn't. It's right here."

"I mean the one for me!"

Ms. Harper looks blankly at me. "Charlotte, this is a two-person job. Sophie is the head; you're the tail."

I'm a WHAT? My mouth drops open.

Sophie nods. "C'mon."

I drag my feet behind her. This can't be happening. I'm supposed to be a horse, not a . . . I can't even say it.

Inside the fitting room, Aubrey is already practicing sitting at the makeup area. She's fluffing up her costume's sleeves as high as they'll go, saying, "Look! It doesn't even fall! They won't go down!"

"Let's go in there, okay?" I say, gesturing to the other room.

Sophie nods.

I sit on the bench and sort through the pieces in my stack. There's a pair of shimmery purple pants with horse hooves built in at the bottom. I pull them on under my tree costume. My feet look like a stuffed animal's. I wish I could wear something beautiful onstage. Just once. But maybe this horse costume won't be so bad. At least the hooves are comfortable. I slip out of the robe and pull on my T-shirt.

Sophie picks up the purple horse head and sighs. "Are you ready?"

I nod.

"Okay, hold the end, would you?" She puts on the horse head. "Okay, now you go under the fabric."

Oh my gosh, it has a tail. A long, purple one covered in glitter, of course. I duck under the fabric, and it settles over us like a tablecloth. I giggle trying to picture what we look like.

"Charlotte! You're supposed to bow down. Your head can't be sticking up. We look like a camel!"

I laugh again. "Okay, okay." I bend at the waist and feel the fabric drape across my back. "Ugh, I can't see anything. Do you think it looks weird?"

A squeal of laughter rings through the air. I know that voice. I stumble out from under the fabric right as Sophie takes off the horse head. Aubrey stands with her hands on her hips, looking like one of those princess cakes from when we were little. She covers her face with her hands and squeals again. "This is the best thing I've ever seen! Don't take it off," she says with a smirk. "You look ridiculous!"

Sophie stuffs the horse head under her arm. She turns to me. "C'mon, Charlotte."

"Maybe you were cast as the wrong witch," I say without a backward glance as we walk out the door. I hear several girls say "Ooooh" as the door shuts behind us, as if I've said something unforgivable.

"Oh my gosh, Charlotte! What's gotten into you?" Sophie says.

I shrug. "I guess I'm a horse's butt."

We both crack up while we wait for Ms. Harper to finish with a group of Munchkins. Ms. Bishop is busy adjusting sleeves on the Scarecrow while at least six other kids try walking around in the shoes she picked out for them.

I still wish I had a role where I could at least get a little glammed up, but watching the other kids get into their costumes reminds me that every role is important. And I'm going to be the best apple tree and horse's butt there ever was.

When it's finally our turn, Ms. Harper says, "Oh, come on! Let's see the whole thing!"

Sophie puts on the horse head, and I bend at the waist under the fabric.

Ms. Harper claps. "This is great! You two are just wonderful. Hang on. . . ." She adjusts the fabric on one side. "Aaah, you need to see this. Hang on, don't move." There's a click, and then she says, "Okay, Sophie, can you see out of that thing?"

"Yes," comes Sophie's muffled voice.

"Perfect. How are you doing, Charlotte? I hope you're not claustrophobic!"

I snicker. It's pitch-black under here, but if I look down, I can see my feet. "I'm okay."

"Can you two walk around a bit? Just to see how it's going to work and make sure the costume doesn't need adjustments?"

Sophie says, "Ready? Just go straight?"

"Yeah."

"Go." We take a few steps together. This is actually working! I keep my eyes on my shiny purple hooves, and I can see exactly where I—

Sophie comes to a sudden stop, and I keep going. The impact makes Sophie pitch forward, and I tumble after her, landing in a tangled heap in the wardrobe closet. Our hooves stick out in every direction.

"Charlotte!" Sophie says, laughing.

"Ugh, I'm sorry," I say as I pick up my glasses and hold them up to the light to make sure they're not cracked. "I didn't know you had stopped!"

Sophie helps me up. "That's okay. We'll get it next time."

Ms. Harper rushes over. "Are you two okay?"

"Fine," I say sheepishly.

"Yeah, I'm okay," Sophie says, rubbing her elbow.

Ms. Harper takes the horse head with the attached fabric and places it back on the table. "I think that move needs some work."

Sophie and I exchange glances and grin. This part will be a lot of fun if we can work on our coordination.

"The extra practice will be so worth it. Check out how great you two look!" She fiddles with her phone and holds up the screen, beaming at us.

The teeth are big and cartoonish, the huge eyes have mile-high fake eyelashes, and with the shimmery light purple fabric draped over us and the deep purple hooves . . . we look like a My Little Pony reject. I laugh. "The audience is going to love it!"

"They will, won't they?" Sophie says with a big smile.

Ms. Bishop places a few pairs of shoes back on the shelves. "Well! There you are!" she says to someone in the hall. "Let's see!"

Aubrey's dress is so poufy, she can hardly fit through the door.

"Aaaaah! Look at her, Ms. Harper!" Ms. Bishop squeals.

"The fit is amazing," Ms. Harper says.

And then Aubrey twirls, like a little kid does in a fancy dress.

"Oh, wait!" Ms. Harper says. "You're missing this!" She strolls over to a table and picks up the most beautiful crown I've ever seen. It's small and delicate, with an elaborate swirl design on every square inch. The crown is topped with bursts of interwoven stars and flowers all around the edge. It's spectacular. She gently lowers the crown onto Aubrey's head, where it catches every color and shimmers in the light. "Take a look," Ms. Harper says. "It's really something."

Aubrey takes in her appearance in the mirror. She stands up straighter and holds her head high. A smile curls at the edges of her lips.

"Mirror, mirror, on the wall," I whisper. "Who's the fairest—"

Sophie elbows me in the side and giggles.

Aubrey makes eye contact with me in the mirror, and

then she smiles so big, I think that sparkle in her eye during the car commercial might be real.

She really does make a good Glinda.

"Hey, Ms. Harper! They need Grace in the office," Jack calls.

Since when does Grace get called to the office? I thought that was just me.

Jack steps into the wardrobe closet and takes in Aubrey in her pink satin and taffeta glory. "Whoa." And in that word, I hear everything I'm not. *The perfect Glinda.* But then he glances at me next to Sophie and says, "Oh my gosh, you two look awesome!" He laughs. "I can't wait to see the whole costume!"

I'm the best horse's butt of all time, and that's more than I was a month ago.

## CHAPTER NINETEEN

# A MILLION LETTERS

I write letters during lunch, class changes, and homeroom. I address them to everyone I can think of who can help us: TV stations, radio stations, every newspaper in the state. I even write the governor! The word spread through our class, and now everyone is writing. Something is going to happen. I can't explain it. It's like the air before a storm, when it crackles with electricity and you can *feel* the change coming. They can't ignore all of us. Then maybe, just maybe, I'll get a chance to play more roles than a shrubbery and a rear end.

I think about Maddie all the time, and what it must have been like to have tea with a pop star last week. I think about Ben, and how we even got here. I think about how Lyric won't talk to me because she thinks she's not supposed to talk to sixth graders, and how ridiculous that is. If it doesn't make sense, why do it? All it does is make other people feel bad. I've felt bad ever since school started. And I am *tired* of feeling bad.

I think that's why I'm writing so many letters to save musical theater. At least I'm doing something about the situation. And writing a note to Ben was a small thing, but I felt so good afterward that I sent even more out into the world. Writing makes me feel better. At first I just wanted to help, but every time I write a note, I'm a little less afraid. This is weird, but . . . it's changing the way I see other kids. I don't think anyone is as confident as they pretend to be.

I wish I could tell every kid that things are going to be okay, that they can survive anything. That they're awesome, that they have the best laugh when they're not worried about hiding their braces, that they mean the world to someone just by being in it.

One note at a time, I'm going to try. I pull out my notebook and put my whole heart into it.

"Charlotte!"

I stop brushing my teeth for a second. "Yeah?"

"Come downstairs! Hurry!" Dad says.

The last time my parents shouted upstairs this early, they

surprised me with pancakes. I rinse my mouth out, grab my backpack, and hustle down the stairs as fast as I can.

Mom's leaning over his shoulder and looking at something on the counter.

"What is it?"

They step away and reveal the front section of the newspaper flipped open. Definitely not pancakes.

I rush over. It's the Letter to the Editor section! I start to read:

*Dear Editor,*

*My name is Aubrey Russell, and I am a seventh grader at Carol Burnett Middle. I'm going to be in a musical this year for the eleventh time. It might also be the last time I'm in a middle school production, because they're taking away musical theater! They say it's so we can have a reading enrichment program, and a bunch of the teachers have to teach it. But we already read in our other classes. And we read in musical theater—how do you think we memorize our lines?*

*Please help tell our story so that maybe, just maybe, whoever's in charge will change their minds. I know I'm just a kid, but I hope you believe me when I tell you that we need this class. We don't take big tests in musical theater, so no one thinks it's important. There's just us, a stage, and all the work we do in between the beginning* *and opening night. But we put our whole hearts into it. The only way you'll understand is if you come and see for yourself. We're performing <u>The Wizard of Oz</u> in one week, October 18–20. Hope to see you there.*

*Yours truly,*

*Aubrey Russell*

My heart races so fast, there's a thudding in my ears. Heat flames in my face. My letter. She sent *my* letter to the editor and the newspaper published it under her name! I mean, I did say my classmates could use it as an example to help them write letters, but I didn't mean they could copy me word for word! I want to scream. How could she do this? It was the one thing that was *mine*.

"What's wrong, Charlotte?" Mom asks. "We thought you'd be happy."

"I would be, but that's my letter. I wrote it. And she . . ." I don't have the energy to finish. Why can't anything ever work out for me? Just once. Would it be so terrible if I finally got a chance to shine?

Dad squeezes my shoulder.

Mom says, "Your letter?"

I nod. "I shared it because I thought it would help the kids in musical theater to see an example. I guess it's my own fault. I just wanted to do something."

"And you *did*."

Dad says, "It might not be your name in the paper, but those are your words. People are going to be talking about this now."

"And that's exactly what you wanted," Mom adds.

"Yeah, I guess you're right." But it doesn't look the way I pictured it.

By now, Ben's almost-bald spot has grown back enough that it's not noticeable anymore. Everything is almost back to normal, except for me and Maddie.

I sit alone on the bus, scribbling on as many pieces of paper as I can. No one would ever know that I used to sit with Maddie, or what I did. I glance over at Lyric, who writes slowly in pink gel pen. When she meets my gaze, she turns her back to me so I can't see what she's doing.

That's fine. I don't want anyone to see my letters. Letters to important people. Letters to kids. Tiny, random notes to leave for someone who needs them. I try to think of the things I wish someone would say to me, and I jot them down as fast as I can:

You are so smart.

I think you could change the world.

*There's someone who thinks you're amazing, and you don't even know it.*

I tear some of the notes into squares, fold them up, and stick them into my pocket.

On the way to homeroom, I slip the folded-up notes into random lockers lining the hallway. The rest of the notes are still in the pages of my binder.

But when I turn the corner, it's so crowded that I can hardly get through. "What's going on?" I ask a random girl pushing past me.

"It's Maddie Hobson. She's telling everyone what celebrities are like!"

"How do you know?"

She flashes her phone. "I got a text!"

Just ahead, I can make out Maddie in the middle of all those kids. Aubrey stands to her left, hanging on every word, along with the rest of the older middle schoolers. Is this real life?

I squeeze through the hallway as quickly as I can, and when I'm almost to my homeroom door, some girl's elbow catches my arm and I drop my binder. Papers fly everywhere, quickly disappearing under students' feet. I duck down and gather them up as quickly as I can. I'm leaning over into the main traffic when there's a tap on my shoulder. Tristan kneels next to me, holding out several pages. His blue eyes are full of guilt and hope all rolled into one. It's the same thing I see when I look at myself.

I gape at him for what feels like forever before I manage to say, "Thanks."

"You're welcome," he says, his face reddening slightly.

I glance at the pages he hands me, and my heart sinks. They're covered in my secret notes to kids. I know he saw them. How could he not have? I hope he doesn't say anything.

We both rise to our feet as the warning bell rings.

"I . . . um . . . see you later," he says. He hesitates, almost as though he wants to say something else, but then he doesn't say any more.

This is so weird. "See you later," I say, trying to sound cool. I walk into homeroom totally stunned. If it hadn't just happened to me, I would never believe it. Tristan actually did something nice! And he did it where everyone could see. I sink into my seat. This sort of thing doesn't just happen, does it? I know I gave him some lunch money, but that was weeks ago. He wouldn't be going out of his way to help me now just because of that. Unless . . . I sit up straighter. I *know* he read my note to him. What if my words actually helped him like I'd hoped?

If one note can do that for one person, there are so many more notes I need to put out in the world. I pull out a fresh piece of paper and write:

*Someone would be so lucky to have a friend like you.*

*You are more than enough.*

*Go be awesome.*

When we go to the library in English, I open a book that I see kids reading all the time, and I tuck a note into the first chapter. I leave one in each of my classes, in empty seats, on the small shelf under some desks, in open backpacks in the hallway. In social studies, I write more notes while Ms. Yang locates the Sahara Desert on a map.

*I hope you see something so beautiful today, it takes your breath away.*

*You matter.*

*Whatever it is, you're going to get better at it. Keep trying!*

Ms. G calls me out of PE. I hurl my bag into the corner of her office and drop into the cracked plastic chair in front of her desk.

"Rough day?"

"Different kind of day." No one is who I think they are. Tristan, Maddie. Who else is going to surprise me today?

"Oh! I brought this for you!" She hands me a newspaper clipping and beams. "It's the most amazing letter! Did you know—"

"Yes."

"So you saw it?"

"Yeah." I sigh.

"I thought you'd be excited about it, Charlotte! Think of all the people who will probably come to the show after reading that letter!"

"I know."

She shakes her head. "Well, I think it's wonderful, and I hope you get to keep performing—if that's what you want!"

"I do want that."

She knows there's something wrong. She has the same look in her eye that my mom has had since this whole mess started with Maddie. "Why don't you tell me what's really bothering you?"

I wish I could. I shrug, my eyes glued to my feet. Maybe I could tell her. What's the worst that could happen? She might understand.

She studies me a moment. "Let me know if you change your mind. You can talk to me."

Why do I always have to get so hot when I'm upset? The

heat rushes to my face, but I don't cry. My anger spills over, and the words come pouring out. "It's *my* letter. I wrote it!"

She gasps. "You?"

I nod and push the letter back across her desk. "I gave it to the k-kids in my class to use as an example for their own letters. She wasn't supposed to steal it!"

"How much did she take? Part of it? Most of it?"

"Almost every word." I clench my jaw. How do I even tell her what that means to me? Would she understand? When you're afraid of your own voice, you're left with the words you put on paper. It's the only time you can make sure they come out the way you want them to. Aubrey stole my *words*.

"Oh, Charlotte." Ms. Garrett shakes her head. "I'm so sorry. That's terrible."

I stare at a spot on her wall. "Thanks."

She says, "Do the other kids know the letter was yours?"

I scoff. "Yes! They *all* know!" My eyes flood with tears, which makes me even madder. I don't want to cry over this. The tears drip onto my jeans, leaving dark splatters. "You know what Aubrey said at the auditions?"

"I'm afraid to ask."

"She said I shouldn't be disappointed when I don't get cast as Glinda." I shake my head. "I didn't think I would, and she doesn't know that I'm in speech or anything. It's just . . . It was—"

"A rotten thing to say. Don't you listen to a word of it."

Ms. Garrett passes me a box of tissues. "And this letter . . ." She sighs.

I take a handful of tissues and blow my nose.

"It's not fair and it's not right." She studies the newspaper clipping. "You really have quite the voice, Charlotte."

I look up at her, my heart fluttering with hope. "You think so?"

She smiles. "I know so. And no matter what anyone says or does, it's unmistakably *yours*."

The tears come again, but this time for a totally different reason. I wipe my face.

"What do you say we get started so you can have a voice onstage, too?" Ms. G asks.

I smile the kind of smile that reaches up my tearstained cheeks all the way to my eyes.

We make it halfway through the play before the bell rings.

Ms. Garrett closes the script and says, "I hope your day gets better. And don't you stop writing letters!"

I nod shyly and exit her office. Something tells me she'd approve of *all* the letters I've been writing. As I make my way to musical theater in the packed hallway, I catch a snippet of conversation between two older boys in front of me. The taller one says, "It's just so random. I opened my locker, and there was this note." He hands it to the shorter boy, who reads aloud, " 'Everyone's pretending to be someone they're not. Just be you'?"

I gasp. I haven't heard anyone talk about my notes.

"That's it," the taller boy says. "Like, who would do that?"

The shorter boy hands the note back to him. "And why did they give it to you?"

"No clue."

I smile and slip inside the auditorium, where Aubrey stands center stage and everyone fights for her attention. My smile fades away. I drop into a seat in the darkened room and wait for the bell. When it chimes, Ms. Harper says, "Before we get started, there's something I want to bring to your attention if you haven't already heard about it." She unfolds today's newspaper.

"'Dear Editor, my name is Aubrey Russell, and I am a seventh grader at Carol Burnett Middle. . . .'"

*La-la-la, can't hear you. Not listening.* I try to picture kids' faces lighting up over my notes, while Ms. Harper continues to read the rest of Aubrey's—*my*—letter. Finally it's over. Ms. Harper says, "Never have I had a student use their writing abilities to do something like this. This was . . . such a nice surprise. And it just goes to show what you can do when you put your mind to it. Now that it's out there, who knows! We may get our miracle." She beams at Aubrey. "You took a chance, and chances are everything. Let's give Aubrey a big hand, folks!"

I clap once. That's it. Everyone else claps and cheers.

She's hugging Jack. How could he do that when he knows I wrote it? The palms of my hands push together just like my teeth are grinding right now. Anyone who read my letter in the group message—and they *all* read it—knows it's mine. So why are they clapping for her? Don't they remember? But as I scan their faces, I catch Grace, Sophie, and several others frowning at Aubrey. Grace leans over to Sophie and mutters something. Sophie nods.

"And—starting Monday, it's tech week!" Ms. Harper continues. "For those of you new to musical theater, listen up! We will meet in full costume daily, with all lights and sound. You should treat each day just like you would a real performance. Something tells me that after the letter in today's paper, we're going to have even more people in the audience than usual. Let's make it count!"

Aubrey places her hand over her heart and sighs.

Sophie and Grace make their way over to me as everyone keeps chattering about the newspaper.

"That's *your* letter!" Sophie says as soon as they reach me.

I nod. "I know. My parents showed it to me this morning."

"We should tell Ms. Harper," Grace says with her hands on her hips.

I shake my head. "No, I don't—"

"We need our Dorothy onstage," Ms. Harper calls out. Grace gives me a look and then turns to go to her mark.

Sophie plops down in a seat near me, opens her script, and sighs.

"Okay," Ms. Harper says. "Let's take it from the beginning. Ready, Ms. Bishop?"

Ms. Bishop plays the opening of the show on the piano, and they begin.

I pull out my notebook and do the only thing I can think of right now. I write more notes.

## CHAPTER TWENTY

# MAKE YOUR MARK

My favorite part about tech week is seeing all the pieces coming together as we prepare for opening night. Seeing everyone in costumes makes us even more focused—our audience will be here before we know it! My classmates are all so talented. They can sing, dance, and act, which Ms. Harper says is a triple threat. I wish I could do that. And the thing is, if I had the chance to get more experience, I think I could! Well, maybe except for the whole dancing part. Let's not go overboard.

While everyone else does their hair and makeup, I have it easy. No makeup needed, and all I have to do is pull my hair back. I'm done in two minutes flat, as opposed to Aubrey, who needs at least twenty minutes. Her hair is off-the-charts huge. She has to put enormous curls in it with so much hair spray, it doesn't move when she walks. Seriously. If a fly landed in it, it would die for sure.

I do the best I can in all my scenes. I work on my timing, and practice moving at the same speed as Sophie in the horse costume. We keep getting better with each rehearsal. I've only knocked her over once since we tried it on the first time!

What doesn't get better is my aim when I throw apples. I don't get it. Sophie's apples roll beautifully to the opposite side of the stage. But mine land everywhere they're not supposed to go—the audience, backstage, Dorothy's head. . . . It's not like I'm trying to do any of that. I've never been able to throw straight in my whole life, so why would anyone think it would be a good idea for me to throw fake apples? They don't go anywhere near as far as real apples would, which I guess is a good thing, since I really don't want to knock Dorothy out.

Ms. Harper takes me aside midway through the week. "Charlotte, we've got to do something about those apples."

"I know. I'm trying."

"Are you nervous?"

"No, I just—I'm trying really hard to stay on that tiny X on the stage, and I keep thinking of what my lines are ahead of time." I'm also thinking about everyone else's lines that I know so well, but she doesn't need to know that.

She nods. "I want you to try this the next time you're onstage."

"Okay."

"Hit your mark, look 'em in the eye, and tell the truth."

"What?" Ms. G wants me to look everyone in the eye, too!

"That's all you have to do. You do that, and it's going to be so much better."

That makes zero sense. I still can't throw worth a flip. "But what about the apples?"

"It was never really about the apples," she says with a wink. "It's about what's going on in your head when you throw them. Just be the tree."

It sounds so simple when she puts it like that. *Just be the tree, Charlotte. Gosh.*

After dinner, I'm helping Mom with the dishes when she casually says, "How's Maddie?"

I take a wet plate from her and dry it. "She's fine. No one's bugging her anymore. All they want to do is meet her new rock star friends."

Mom hands me another plate. "Wonder what she thinks about that."

I place the dry plate in the stack to put back into the cabinet. "That she lived happily ever after?"

"She's a smart girl, Charlotte. She has to know those kids are talking to her for the wrong reasons."

"I d-don't think that matters to her. She's like the most popular kid in school now."

"Of course it matters." She rinses the last plate and hands it to me. "Charlotte . . . friendships like yours don't just end overnight. I know it feels like it, but I think you might be surprised."

She'd be shocked to find that friendships can end in even less time. Like half a second. I dry the dishes in silence and put them in the cabinet. "I'm going to my room."

"Have you tried talking to her again?" she calls when I'm almost around the corner. "Her mom thinks you should."

I stop in my tracks and glance over my shoulder at her. "You talked to Maddie's mom?!" My voice comes out higher-pitched on the last word.

"Of course I did."

"What—" My stomach flips. "What did she say?"

She wipes the countertop. "Just that you need to call Maddie."

I shake my head and bolt upstairs as fast as I can. Maddie hasn't responded to my letter. What makes our moms think she'd talk to me on the phone?

Once I reach my room, I close the door and hurl myself onto my bed. I glance over at the phone on my dresser. I could call Maddie. What's one more try? I frown. Unless I can't get the words out again. The only way I can make sure they come out right is if I write them. I'm out of options.

I need to feel like I'm making a difference, to fix something outside myself. Writing is the only thing that makes me feel that way. So I write three more letters to the rest of the school board to try to distract myself. Do they even care what some kid thinks? I hope so. If I've learned anything at all this year, it's that if you don't say what's important to you, you miss your chance. Maddie is gone. I can't let musical theater pass me by, too. As I seal the last letter, I think maybe it doesn't matter if the people in charge don't want to listen. If enough of us write, they're going to hear us whether they want to or not.

I know my other notes have been heard. I saw Ben smile. Tristan helped me in the hallway, and even though it happened a while after I left the note for him, I think my words meant something to him. Aubrey definitely thinks she's shining as Glinda, but honestly, that note was more about me trying to be a good sport. I don't know what Josh thought about his note, but at least I tried. But the one I want to know about most is my letter to Maddie. I hoped so hard that it would fix what I'd broken, but there's nothing. No response. No sign that she even got it. But she *had* to have gotten it. My mom probably made sure of it when she talked to Maddie's mom.

I pick up my pen, and all the words I wish I could say to myself and other kids come pouring out:

It's going to get better.

You're not alone.

I love talking to you because you're awesome.

You're making a big difference.

I write page after page, thought after thought. It's silly, but I try to make each sentence a hug. Maybe it will help someone.

You have the best smile.

I'm rooting for you.

It's okay to cry. We all do it.

Make it count.

I think for a second, and then add one more line to the notes I've written:

*Being brave means doing the right thing even when you're scared. Be brave anyway.*

I should follow my own advice.

In English, we skip reading novels and move straight to writing. I flip open my journal and find that Ms. Harper has been reading my work again. On my page about speaking up, Ms. Harper wrote, *This is more like it, Charlotte! ☺ I knew you had it in you! Keep writing!*

In my journal entry about kid celebrities, she wrote, *I wonder what made you write about this. I think there must be a story there—maybe a short story. Find the heartbeat. Can you feel it?*

No, I can't. You have to have a heart for that. Ugh, I'm completely out of writing ideas. I've written about the most ridiculous stuff, and none of it has been real except for the essay about speaking up for what I believe in. Ms. Harper liked that one for a reason.

I take a deep breath. Ms. Harper wants me to find the heartbeat. I guess that means I need to show her what's in my awful heart. What was that she said? Oh yeah. *Hit your mark, look 'em in the eye, and tell the truth.*

This is my truth. Here goes nothing.

With a steadier hand than I thought I'd have, I write:

Have you ever done something so bad, you couldn't take it back?

I have. I hurt a friend to protect myself.

There are all these moments that happened so fast, each one worse than the one before. It was like watching a line of dominoes topple over, and once the fall started, it was too late. There was no going back.

You might say, "Wow, Charlotte, what were you thinking? How could you have done something like that?"

That's what I would have thought if I'd been there watching it happen. I'd think, I would never do such a thing. I'd stop it.

And yet, here I am. I never stopped it. I stepped out of the way.

I didn't even think about it. I made a choice. A terrible choice to not do anything at all, because doing something would hurt me too much. But friendship doesn't work that way.

I've felt awful for weeks now because I did nothing. And when you keep doing nothing, it just gets worse.

So I finally did something. Not a big something that might make anything close to the way it was, but a bunch of little somethings that might make the world a tiny bit better for someone. I also started the letter-writing campaign to save musical theater. The letter in the newspaper was mine.

I hope that counts in the whole scheme of things. I don't know what else to do.

"Time's up!" Ms. Harper says.
I hope not.

"So, tonight's the night?" asks Ms. G when we're sitting in her office.

"Yeah." I've been queasy since last night, and my stomach is in total knots today. I can't believe opening night is already here.

"Are you nervous?"

"No." Yes.

"You're going to be great."

I shrug it off. "It's not like I have a lot to d-d"—I pause and take a breath—"do."

"There are no small parts."

"Just small horses."

She laughs. "Let's get started. I guess we'll need to find a new play after this one, won't we?"

"Maybe." That would be okay with me.

We start at the beginning. She sits in her swivel chair, the manuscript in her hands, and I read all the good parts. I know every line. Every action. Everything. And I say it all while looking her right in the eye.

When the bell rings, she claps and cheers. My cheeks burn, but it feels really good to hear applause. I don't think I've ever performed and been clapped for in my entire life.

She says, "Break a leg!"

I grin. "Thanks!"

I take my time going to the auditorium. By this time tomorrow, opening night will be over with, and I'll always get to say that I was part of it. That's something. I've also managed to scatter every single note I have all over the school. They're in lockers, in backpacks, on seats, in bathrooms. I put a few more in library books. It makes me smile to think of someone opening a book and reading something kind stuck between the pages. Leaving a note only takes a second, just like the Bad Thing only took a second. And with each note, I wonder how many it would take to make up for what I did to Maddie. If you put enough good into the world, does it cancel out the bad you've done?

I walk through the auditorium doors, and the full stage

lights are already on. Ms. Harper is adjusting the sound levels. This is it. Our last run-through.

The rehearsal goes just like it's gone every day this week, except I'm *finally* spot-on with the silly apples. I don't even think about where I'm throwing them. Trees don't think about their aim. They just think about making Dorothy go away. As for the horse, Sophie and I have it down. When we hear the line about the horse being a different color, Sophie and I both prance and neigh, and we exit the stage. Everyone seems to think it's great, and I'm having a blast!

"Listen up," Ms. Harper says. "Be back at five-thirty sharp! I know that's not much time, but we have a lot to do to get ready, and we can't be late. Try not to overuse your voices this afternoon. Glinda's understudy just came down with laryngitis, and we need everyone healthy tonight! Yes?"

We nod.

She continues, "I will see you all *very* soon!" Then her eyes meet mine, and the space between her eyebrows wrinkles. She frowns and turns away.

That's not like her. Was I not very good today? Maybe she talked to Ms. Garrett and she's worried that I'll stutter onstage. That's what *I'm* worried about.

"Hey, Aubrey," Ms. Harper calls. "I need to speak with you a moment."

My eyes widen. Or *maybe* Ms. Garrett told Ms. Harper that I wrote the letter! I don't really mind if she did. Ms.

Harper will know everything after she reads my journal. It's my truth, not Aubrey's.

The bell rings, and I steal a glance over my shoulder. Aubrey approaches Ms. Harper, who holds a newspaper in her hand, and Ms. Bishop joins them. They look so serious.

"Do you think anyone will come?" I ask Grace, Sophie, and Jack as we step into the sunshine. It's cool outside, and I catch a whiff of woodsmoke in the air. It smells like fall.

"Are you kidding? The whole town will be here because the plays are always so good," says Grace.

"No, no. I mean all the people we wrote those letters to."

"Oh, I hope so," says Sophie. "They have to see it to get it."

"They'll be here, especially after Aubrey's letter ran in the paper. Oh yeah. Just you wait," Jack says.

Grace shakes her head. "Actually, it's—"

I elbow Grace, and she sighs. "Never mind," she says, exchanging a knowing glance with Sophie.

I know it's *my* letter, but I don't even want to bring it up now. I just hope all our hard work means something. We tried to save musical theater class. How many other kids can say that?

"See you later," I say, and climb up the bus steps.

Scanning the seats for an empty spot, I stiffen. Josh is in the seat across the aisle from Maddie, his shoulders turned in her direction. My already-nervous stomach plummets.

Where are the kids who were chatting with her last week? They're nowhere near her. Neither is Lyric, who's sitting near my usual spot, but that's no surprise. I study Maddie's face as I get closer. She doesn't look upset, really—more like she's bracing herself for the worst. She's in the seat by the window, but her bag is in the spot next to the aisle. I keep going.

*It's never too late to do the right thing.*

I slide into the seat behind her so no one else can. Just in case. They're not going to sit behind her and torment her anymore as long as I'm around.

A moment later, Tristan plops down in the seat in front of Maddie. He turns to Josh across the aisle and doesn't even look at Maddie.

I lean back when I spot a small square of folded notebook paper next to me. That's weird. I didn't see it there when I sat down. I pick it up, unfold it, and read a message in pink gel pen:

You're not done yet. :) Keep going.

Whoa! Who wrote this?

I sit up straighter. No one is glancing my way. They're all looking out the windows, reading, talking to other people, or playing on their phones. Who could it be? I steal a glance at Lyric, whose gaze meets mine when she looks up from writing something in a notebook. She rolls her eyes and turns her back to me. No, it's definitely not her, I realize with a twinge of disappointment. If she had written this note, it would mean there's still a part of her that's my friend, but I know that's not true.

I look back down at the note. Someone copied me, but they didn't do it like Aubrey did. They didn't steal my words. They wrote their own and put them out there for kids who might need them. *I* need them.

I refold the note and put it into my shirt pocket, right over my heart.

## CHAPTER TWENTY-ONE

# A SHOE-IN!

The parking lot is completely full. Cars are parked on the sidewalk, in the bus loading dock, and even in the teachers' parking spaces.

Families dot the sidewalks as they walk toward the building.

My heart pounds. This is it. People are actually going to be watching me throw apples and prance around as a horse. I feel sick and giddy at the same time.

Dad pulls our SUV up to the sidewalk. "Why don't you all go get tickets, and I'll try to find a place to park?"

I don't need to be told again. I tumble out of the car in record time.

Mom shuts the door, and we walk in together.

"You're going to be fine," she says.

I smile. "I know."

"I'm proud of you for doing this."

I reach over and pat her shoulder. "I love you, Mom." No way am I going to hug her in front of everyone. It would be too embarrassing. "Hey, what time is it?"

Mom checks her phone. "It's five-twenty-eight."

"Oh no! Gotta run!"

"Go get 'em, kiddo!" Mom says, raising her fist in the air when she says it.

I dart away as fast as possible. Right in front of the auditorium, I gape at the crowd. There are parents with kids, grandparents, and a bunch of teachers. Is this normal? Would they have turned out like this anyway? Or . . . did we do this with our letters?

Everything backstage is a blur of fabric and powder. Every light illuminates the front dressing room. The girls with the biggest roles sit at the counter putting on their makeup and doing their hair. I move on to the next room, where Sophie is chatting with several girls who play Munchkins. I slip into my tree costume robe just like I've done every day this week. After I pull my hair back into a low ponytail, I wipe my glasses on my sleeve, then put them back on. Done. I fold up my regular clothes and put them into my locker. With the star on it. But there's a folded square of paper right at the edge of the locker door. I unfold it, and in familiar pink gel pen it reads *Go Big or Go Home*. I scan the fitting room, but no one is even looking my way. If anyone here put it in my locker, they're not acting like it. Is the note for *me*? Or could it be for anyone, and I just happened to find it? I have so many questions! But that reminds me. I reach into the pocket of my folded jeans, pull out the other note that I found on the bus, and slip it into a locker several spaces down from mine. Maybe someone else in the play needs it, too.

"Hey, Charlotte!" Grace says, poking her head around the corner, already in her gingham blue dress, with bare feet.

"Hey, superstar!"

"Oh, please," she says. But her face glows with happiness. "Nervous?"

"More excited than anything else. Are you?"

"Are you kidding? I've been waiting for this my whole life."

I grin. I know exactly what she means.

"WHOA!" Sophie yells.

We all turn to see her looking down at her phone.

"Check this out! My mom just sent it!" She holds up a picture of the auditorium, with crowds of people everywhere. It's packed.

I squeeze Grace's arm, and we all jump up and down and squeal.

The entire room buzzes with excitement. We might actually save musical theater class if we have enough support. We have one weekend to wow everyone with this play. *One.*

We move into the front dressing room just as Aubrey stands in costume in front of the full-length mirror, Grace's slippers in hand.

"What do you think you're doing?" Grace says.

"Relax. I'm just trying them on. I want to see what they look like." She holds on to the counter and puts one shoe on.

Grace crosses the room in record time and grabs the other slipper, still in Aubrey's hand. "I don't think so. You could stretch them out. Or scuff them. I don't want anything to happen before we go on!"

Aubrey tugs on the shoe, but Grace doesn't let go. I never thought I'd see Dorothy and Glinda in a real-life showdown over slippers.

"Give me my shoe!" Grace says. "This isn't all about you, you know."

"Oh, don't be such a baby! It's just a shoe."

Grace's eyes widen. "Oh yeah? Like it was just a letter in the newspaper?"

Aubrey clenches her jaw.

Grace continues, "Did you think no one noticed?" Then she turns to the whole room. "Listen up, everybody," she says, gesturing with her open arms. "You know how Aubrey wrote a letter to the paper? Just in case you forgot—it was Charlotte's! She was nice enough to share it to help us write our letters!"

Everyone stares and nods.

Aubrey tugs at the shoe again, but Grace is never letting go of it.

"So now that we've reminded everyone that you like to take things that aren't yours, how about letting go of my shoe?"

Ms. Harper bursts into the dressing room. "WHAT is going on in here?" she says, rushing over to Aubrey.

We all exchange glances.

"Speak!"

I step forward. "They were fighting over the shoes."

Ms. Harper's expression doesn't change. It's like she didn't hear me. "What?"

"She was trying to take my shoes, Ms. Harper!"

Aubrey holds her chin up, like she's daring Grace to say another word.

"Shoes," Ms. Harper says, with an icy chill to her voice. "I need to speak with you in the hallway, Aubrey. *Now.*" Her face turns splotchy and red. I've never seen her so upset.

"You should've just let me try them on," Aubrey says, glaring at Grace.

"Not another word," Ms. Harper says. Her gaze falls on Aubrey's slippered foot. "Give me the shoe, please," she says, holding out her hand.

Grace's eyes meet Aubrey's as though to say, *See? Told you!*

Aubrey presses her lips together and hands the shoe to Ms. Harper.

Ms. Harper passes the slipper to Grace and whisks Aubrey out of the room.

We file out of the dressing room while they disappear out the stage side door. Ms. Bishop should be calling us to our places, but then she disappears out the door, too.

"What do you think will happen?" Sophie asks me.

"If Ms. Harper doesn't have a heart attack?" I ask.

"Yeah."

"I don't know," I say.

Sophie shakes her head. "I can't believe Aubrey."

"Neither can I," says Grace, coming over to stand with us. "Hey, um . . . you don't think it's my fault, do you?"

"No!" we say in unison.

"Maybe I should've just let her have the shoe."

"I'm glad you didn't," Sophie says.

Grace doesn't look so sure.

Jack strolls up to us, the silver funnel securely in place with a clear strap under his chin. "Did I miss something?"

The side door opens, but instead of Ms. Harper, it's Ms. G. In her arm is a small bouquet of flowers. I rush over to her. I don't want anyone to know who she is, but I'm really glad to see her.

"Charlotte! I wanted to swing by and give you these." She hands me the bouquet of flowers. "You're going to be wonderful!"

"Thanks, b-b—" I pause, take a deep breath, and try again as I exhale. "But I'm worried there's not going to be a show."

"What? Why?"

At that moment, Aubrey storms in through the side door. "Because there goes Glinda," I say as quietly as I can.

Ms. G takes in Aubrey's crown in her hand and her mascara-stained cheeks as she slams the dressing room door shut behind her. "Oh *no.*"

"Yeah, I'm not really sure what happened," I say, and then I spill about the shoe fight.

She glances around. "Where's Ms. Harper?"

"Beats me. Probably trying to figure out how to refund everyone's money." So much for our one big chance to show everyone what we can do.

"Isn't there an understudy?" Ms. G asks.

I shake my head. "Yeah, but she's sick!"

Her eyes widen. "Okay. Hang tight," she says. "I'm going to see if I can help."

"Thanks for the flowers," I say.

As soon as she's gone, Grace says, "Who was that?"

Uh-oh. "Um, just this teacher." It's like Grace's eyes are boring holes into me. I wipe my sweaty palms on my tree robe. "She helps me," I add.

"With what?"

I can't stand that they're staring at me. This is too much. Maybe I should just say it. It's not like they haven't heard me stutter a million times already. "Speech."

"Oh, okay," Grace says, but she doesn't sound surprised at all. I knew everyone had noticed. How could they not?

"Yeah." My face feels like it's on fire. My speech isn't something that I talk about. Not even with Maddie. I always pretend I don't do it, and she always pretends not to notice. "I stutter. I have since I was little."

Grace nods. "That's okay. Doesn't everybody do that sometimes?"

"Not like I do. I hate it. That's why I get called out of class sometimes." I steal a glance at Jack, whose warm eyes seem to glitter against his silver stage makeup. He's not laughing.

"You shouldn't be embarrassed," Grace says. "I have to go to the clinic *all* the time!"

"You do?" I remember her getting called out of class one day.

"Yep. The school nurse has to help me check my insulin. I'm diabetic."

"I didn't know that." Maybe everyone is dealing with something, and we just don't know about it.

"Well, now you do."

Ms. Bishop walks briskly through the side door and disappears into the backstage area.

Sophie turns to me and says, "So, like, what do you do when you're onstage? Is it harder?"

"Yeah." I fidget. "I pretty much freak out every single second."

Jack shakes his head. "But you do it anyway! That's awesome."

Grace says, "I never would've known you were nervous."

I look down at my shoes. "You'll know it if I mess up. I'll be known as the girl with the stutter."

"No," Grace says. "You'll still be Charlotte. And *everybody* messes up. We're not on Broadway yet."

And when she squeezes my arm, I know she means it.

Ms. Harper bursts back through the door, her mouth set in a firm line, and makes a beeline for Ms. Bishop. They talk in the corner in hushed voices.

"We have an announcement!" Ms. Harper says. She motions for us to come closer so the people in the audience won't hear what they say.

"The role of Glinda will be played by"—her eyes scan our faces until they lock on mine—"Charlotte Andrews."

Mouths drop open. "Charlotte Andrews?"

"Charlotte Andrews!" someone from the back says.

"Charlotte?" Sophie says.

ME?

## CHAPTER TWENTY-TWO

# SHOWTIME

I'm whisked into the dressing room so quickly that I don't even get a chance to look for Ms. G and find out what she said. But I know she's the reason why the dress of my dreams is slipping over my head. It's like all the colors are somehow brighter than they were a minute ago, but I think a lot of that has to do with the huge lightbulbs above the mirror at each seat. Ms. Bishop pins the hem at the bottom because it's a tad too long.

I sit down at Aubrey's seat, and the fabric poofs up a lot higher than I imagined.

"Glasses, please," Ms. Bishop says.

I hand them over.

"Okay, where's your makeup, Charlotte?" Ms. Harper asks.

"I, um, don't have any."

She turns to everyone in the dressing room. "Girls! Emergency! I need stage makeup! All you've got!"

There's a flurry of movement everywhere as they reach for their cosmetic bags. Ms. Harper digs into a drawer and pulls out a wide-barreled curling iron. "Time to get you Glinda-fied. You ready?"

Yes, yes, so much yes! I nod. "Sure."

"Concealer!"

A small tube appears out of nowhere.

Ms. Harper says, "Hey, Ms. Bishop? Would you see if you can find a replacement for Charlotte's part of the horse? Once her hair is done, there's no changing out of her costume."

"On it!" says Ms. Bishop. "What about the tree?"

"I think we're covered. Hey, Sophie!" Ms. Harper calls. "Is she in here?"

Sophie rounds the corner.

"Can you handle Charlotte's apple tree lines on top of your own?"

"I think so."

"Perfect! That's one thing done."

"Okay, one second half of a horse, coming right up," Ms. Bishop says as she slips out of the dressing room.

"Foundation!" Ms. Harper says, holding out her hand.

A few bottles are passed around until they reach Ms. Harper. "Hmm. That one," she says.

One of the Munchkins starts dabbing it onto my face.

Ms. Harper works on my hair.

"Where'd you learn to do that?" I ask.

"I have a little sister," Ms. Harper says.

"She taught you?"

She laughs. "No. Definitely not. But sometimes she let me practice with her hair if I pestered her long enough." She studies my face. "Blush!"

Four compacts arrive a moment later.

"You kind of remind me of her a bit, actually," Ms. Harper says as she swirls a makeup brush across the powder.

"Really?" I like that.

"Mmm-hmm. Hey, Grace, pass me that hair spray, would you?" She shakes the can four times, and says, "Hold your breath!"

It's like being covered with tree sap that dries crunchy. When she's done spraying down every inch of my hair, she says, "My sister definitely would've written the editor that letter."

I look down. I want to tell her that I wrote it, but I can't make my mouth move.

"Just like you did," she says.

I snap my head up. "You read my journal!" Oh my gosh,

SHE READ MY JOURNAL. The one where I wrote about the Bad Thing. I can't breathe. What must she think of me now?

"Sure did. And I think what you did . . ." She pauses for a moment.

I'm going to die. I'm going to fall right out of this chair, and then they'll be down two Glindas in one night. That has to be some kind of record.

"Sending those letters was remarkable."

Relief pours over me. I can't take credit for this when it was a group effort. That's not fair to everyone else. "We sent the letters, Ms. Harper. All of us."

"But you got that train rolling."

I smile. "Maybe."

"What gave you the idea?" Her blue eyes are kind as she brushes a setting powder across my face.

"I wanted to do more than *write* about standing up for what I believe in. I had to actually *do* it." If Ms. Harper knew the real me, she'd know that writing was the only voice I had before I found the courage to speak onstage. But things are different now.

"I'm glad you did. Oh, and I've been meaning to ask," she says, dusting my eyelids with glittery gold eye shadow. "How would you like to write for the school paper?"

My eyes fly open, narrowly missing the makeup brush. "Are you serious? I thought that was just for seventh and eighth graders!"

She nods. "I'm *so* serious. We could use that voice of yours. And I promise that you'll get credit for your work in this paper!"

I break into a big smile. "It would be nice to know what that's like."

A dab of lip gloss later, and Ms. Harper is beaming. "Don't turn around yet! You still need the accessories. Hey, Sophie, grab that choker, would you?" Ms. Harper lowers the crown onto my head, pins it in place, and sprays that, too! That thing is never coming out of my hair. "Okay," she says, handing me my glasses, "stand up for me." Finally she scoots the shoes in front of me, and once they're on my feet, she hands me the wand. "Go ahead. Look."

My feet barely touch the ground on the way to the full-length mirror. My jaw drops when I see my reflection. Is this real? My usually dull brown hair is shiny, with tons of curls. My cheeks are rosy, my lips shiny, and the whole thing just . . . There's a small catch in my throat. "I look amazing."

Grace says, "C'mon, you *are* amazing." She says it like it's something everyone knows, like cafeteria food is awful.

I stare back at the mirror. This feels like some kind of dream.

Ms. Bishop pokes her head back into the room. "It's time!"

While we trail behind everyone else filing out of the dressing room, I say, "Hey, Ms. Harper?"

"Yeah?"

"I hope I don't screw up the play. I've never done this before." So many people are counting on me now. If I mess this up, it's curtains for musical theater here. No pressure or anything.

She lowers her voice. "That's not what I heard!"

My mouth drops open again. I knew it. I wonder what else Ms. G told Ms. Harper.

"You've got this. I think you earned this role more than anyone else. Just remember to tell 'em the truth. Get out of your own way, Charlotte."

Ha! No one's ever put it quite like that before. I wipe my sweaty palms on the skirt of the dress. "Okay."

As we exit with the rest of the group, she says, "And have fun. Because if it isn't fun, what's the point? It's just a play."

It's so much more than that to me.

She motions for everyone to gather around. "You've worked so hard for this night, and I couldn't be prouder of each and every one of you. And I'm so excited to tell you that we have a *sold-out* show!"

We gasp.

"I know you're hoping for a miracle, and I'd be telling the biggest whopper ever if I told you I'm not hoping for the same. But whatever happens here tonight, I'll never forget this class. For what you did. For reminding me that there's always hope. And for putting so much of yourselves and your incredible hearts and talent into the work. You surprised me at every turn."

Ms. Harper smiles, and it reaches all the way up to her misty eyes. "Now go out there and show this community how amazing you are!" She looks around at all of us, and lands on me when she says, "I'm rooting for you."

My heart feels like it could explode from happiness.

"Places!" Ms. Bishop says. "It's time!"

I try to busy myself backstage by running all of the lines in my head, but that doesn't do anything to make me less nervous. I peek out of a small crack at the edge of the curtain, and I wish I hadn't. I've never seen so many people in an auditorium before! I wouldn't even know where to look to find my parents, but they have to be out there somewhere.

The Kansas part flies by, and before I know it, Dorothy's house has crashed in Oz, and the moment I've waited for forever is finally here. *Don't screw this up, Charlotte! Do not, do not, do not!* It's time to hold my wand high and tell the truth. I'm not Charlotte Andrews. I'm Glinda, and I'm Dorothy's only hope.

I step into the light. I practically float onstage, which is great because I'm technically supposed to be in a bubble, but no way do we have the budget for something like that.

So, they beam the spotlight right on me for effect. Dorothy shrinks back from me a touch, and I ask her the question that defines all of Oz: "Are you a g-good witch, or a bad witch?" And even though I stutter just a bit, I act like it didn't happen. We continue the dialogue until it's time for the Munchkins to come out. This is going to be tricky, but how many times have I sung along to this? How many days did I watch Aubrey prance around onstage? I've never rehearsed Glinda's actions, but I know them by heart. I can so do this.

I open my mouth to sing, and thank goodness, it's fine. It's better than fine. I never stutter when I sing, and I sound *good*! I glide across the stage, giving my wand a gentle wave here and there.

After I point Dorothy toward the Yellow Brick Road, I exit the stage, and a surge of relief and adrenaline washes over me. One scene down; one more to go at the end! I can't believe it went so well.

Sophie rushes up to me in her tree robe and whisper-squeals, "That was awesome!"

I didn't know my smile could ever be this big.

Jack waves from his spot along the wall, his funnel hat on his knee. He's faintly gleaming from the silver shimmer of his costume.

He's actually waving at *me.* I wave back, and out of the

corner of my eye I see my enormous pink sleeve rise. I pick my usual seat next to Sophie's, even though she's onstage right now for the big apple tree scene. Her voice rings out, yelling at Dorothy, and the apples land backstage right in front of us. I've never seen the action like this before!

Jack walks to the curtain to do his big scene. Sophie slides into the seat next to me.

"You were great!" I say. "Check out all those apples!"

"I mean, I guess I am pretty impressive," Sophie says.

We both laugh.

"Gotta run. You know what time it is," Sophie says with a wink.

I smile. I do, indeed. "See ya." Sophie and whoever replaced me will be fine in the horse costume, as long as they have as much coordination as I do.

When the characters reach the Emerald City, the audience cheers for the horse of a different color! There's a lot of laughter, too, but it's because they love the costume so much.

Some of the other kids grin at me in between scenes. One of the eighth graders passes by and whispers, "You wrote an awesome letter, Charlotte!"

My smile stretches from ear to ear.

Sophie returns and removes the horse head. "Whew!"

"How did it go?"

"It wasn't *you*, but we got it done."

Finally it's time. Dorothy clicks her heels together three times, and I am *done*.

When the curtain closes on Dorothy after the final scene, the applause thunders throughout the auditorium. We line up when the curtain reopens, and we all run onto the stage, forming one long line. We hold hands and bow together. Dorothy steps forward, and several people stand up. We bow again, and this time everyone in the audience stands. A standing ovation! For us! Then we all extend our arms to Ms. Bishop, who's standing at the piano. More applause. Finally we gesture toward Ms. Harper with our right arms outstretched, and the applause grows even louder. One of the parents runs forward and gives each teacher a bouquet of roses.

It couldn't be any more perfect. The curtain closes, and in this moment, I feel like I can do anything. Anything at all.

Grace turns and gives me a huge hug. "CHARLOTTE! You did it! That was awesome! Who's the superstar now?"

I hug her back even harder. "You were the best Dorothy."

"Oh, please."

"No, really." When Grace opens her mouth onstage, everyone knows she belongs there.

Ms. Harper walks backstage. "I am so proud of you!" she says. We all rush in for a teary group hug.

When I pop out on the other side of the curtain, cheering erupts from my parents in the second row. I run down the side stage stairs, and as soon as I'm close enough, they throw their arms around me.

"Charlotte!" Mom says, wiping a tear off her cheek. "You were *not* a tree!" She laughs. "Or a horse—I don't think."

"You should've seen her when we realized you were Glinda," Dad says. "She tapped my arm for two minutes straight!" Dad shakes his head and laughs.

"Well, it was a very exciting moment!" She turns to me. "How did it happen?"

"Long story. Can I tell you on the way home?"

"Nope. You can tell us over ice cream! We're going out to celebrate," Mom says.

"Yes!"

Dad says, "The sooner you change, the sooner we'll be eating sundaes!"

"I'm going, I'm going!"

Mom grabs me in another hug, and we jump up and down and cheer.

### CHAPTER TWENTY-THREE

# IT'S A WRAP

On Monday morning, I stroll down the sidewalk toward the bus stop. I walk around an upside-down message in chalk and look over my shoulder to read it.

*Be your own hero*

My heart swells. Kindness finally caught on, and it feels amazing.

Lyric stares at me from the curb. I drop my bag and examine the tic-tac-toe game drawn on the driveway. There's a piece of blue chalk that someone left behind. I think I'll leave a message of my own.

I pick up the chalk and write in big, bold letters:

As I'm finishing filling in the last letters, I feel Lyric's eyes on me. I glance up and find her standing by my bag, studying the words I wrote on the pavement. "What?" I say.

"I didn't say anything."

The bus wheezes up the hill and onto our street. When it's almost here, she nods at my sidewalk art and says, "I just . . . I think it's really nice of you to write that."

I glance up at her and smile.

The bus doors open.

I place the chalk back where I found it, grab my bag, and go up the stairs. I glance toward Maddie, but the seats around her are already full. Ben waves in his usual first seat. "Hey," I say, sliding in next to him.

"Hey," he says. He's holding a library book in one hand and a note in the other.

"What's that?"

"This?" He holds up the note. "It's the weirdest thing. I keep finding these notes. Check it out."

In bright purple ink, it reads:

*Hey, you. Yeah, you. You belong. Really.*

I wish I knew who else was writing notes!

"Charlotte, what is it?" he asks.

"Nothing. I just . . . That's really nice."

"Yeah, I thought so, too."

I found the note in pink gel pen in my bus seat the other day. Then I found another one in my dressing room locker in the same handwriting. But this one was written by someone else. So, there are *two* other people writing notes like mine now?

"I also have this one." He digs into his pocket and hands me another note, this one in neat black ink. It says:

## We all mess up. It's okay.

Oh my goodness. I study one note, and then the other. No way the same person wrote them, which means . . . *three* other people are writing notes? And what about that message on the sidewalk? Did *I* cause this? Is that even possible? I've left so many notes all over the school. Could it be that my words inspired other kids to leave notes of their own?

A small shiver travels up my neck. I did it! Something I wrote was so powerful, other kids heard my voice. I did something that *mattered*. But now I have to figure out how to use my voice to fix things with Maddie. I hand the notes back to Ben.

"It's like all these people decided to speak up at the same time," he says with a shrug. "It's nice and all, but I don't get it."

I say, "Maybe there's nothing to get. Maybe they just wanted to do something good."

"Maybe."

"Hey, Ben?"

"Yeah?"

"Do you remember when you said it was brave of Maddie to snitch?"

He nods.

"I thought about that a lot, and well . . . You know the student writing that Ms. Harper shared in English about speaking up for what you believe in?"

"Yeah."

"I wrote it."

He raises his eyebrows. "Wow, Charlotte. That was really good."

I blush. "Thanks. But I wrote it because I kept thinking about what you said, and I thought it was something I needed to do."

"And did you? Speak up, I mean?" He tucks his notes back inside his library book.

I sneak a peek back at Maddie. Her head is bowed down, and no one is trying to talk to her anymore.

I turn back to Ben. "Not the way I wanted. But I will."

When I get my journal back toward the end of English class, I flip to my last entry as fast as I can and steel myself for Ms. Harper's reply. It says:

*I see you, Charlotte. I see all that you've done, and I can't wait to see all the things you'll do. Keep writing. Write with fire. Write with truth. Write with your whole heart, and don't you stop until you've told your story.*

If it were possible for my heart to fill with happiness and carry me away, it would happen right at this moment. I glance over at Ms. Harper, who's supposed to be writing, but her pen is nowhere near the paper when her eyes meet mine. She beams and gives me a small nod.

I knew words were powerful, but I never knew how much until today. I feel like I could do anything! I've already written with my whole heart and reached Ms. Harper, a newspaper editor, and the kids at my school. If I can do all that, how can I not use my voice to help my best friend?

I lean over my bag to dig for a pen, and my breath stops short. There's a red notebook in my bag, and it wasn't there last night when I did my homework. It is THE red notebook. I've seen it a million times. I place it on my desk and open the cover. There's a sticky note inside that says *in pink gel pen:*

*I ended up with this notebook, and I was so embarrassed that I didn't know how to give it back. I know you'll do the right thing.*

The *I*s are dotted with hearts. The handwriting matches the notes I've found around school! And now I'm pretty sure that I know this writing.

I replay the morning in my mind. I sat with Ben, and before that, I drew on the sidewalk while Lyric watched. I glance back at the note, and my jaw drops when I see a smudge of blue chalk on the paper. Lyric had the notebook all this time? Her weird question about Maddie makes more sense now. Lyric asked if Maddie and I were still friends because she wanted help returning the notebook! And it was *Lyric* sending the random kind notes? Seriously? I just . . . I don't understand. How could she act horrible in person, and then do something like that? I cringe. Probably the same way I did. I was never mean, but I completely messed up. Maybe she was trying to replace some bad with the good, like I tried to do. I don't know. Maybe I'll never know.

I stare at the notebook. I have to give it back to Maddie, I know. I will. And yet, I wonder. Should I look inside?

Maddie never wanted me to read any of her stuff. But what if Lyric gave it to me for a reason? Am I *supposed* to look?

The bell rings.

"See you tomorrow! Make good choices!" Ms. Harper says.

The good choice is not to read the notebook. I can't invade someone's most private thoughts. That would be yet another Bad Thing, and I've had enough of that. I stuff the notebook back into my bag.

I walk through the auditorium doors and make my way down the main aisle. I take a seat next to Grace.

"Hey, superstar," she says.

I laugh. "Maybe in another universe." A few rows up, Aubrey is slumped in her chair. Jack sits beside her, chatting away about all the things she missed during the shows over the weekend. I'll bet she really appreciates that.

The bell rings, but there's no Ms. Harper. After a few minutes, she walks in the back door. "Sorry!" she says. She makes her way to the front. "I've just come from Principal Sinclair's office."

Every single kid leans forward in their seat, and no one dares to speak.

"We had news coverage from the local paper and school board members in attendance." She pauses. "Nice job, you. Give yourselves a big hand for that."

We break into applause, and just as quickly, we stop, eager for her to continue.

"They've definitely heard from the community," she says with a chuckle. "If it were up to everyone at opening night, we'd have musical theater every semester. But unfortunately, they're not the ones choosing where money is spent."

The whole class starts whispering, and Ms. Harper has to shush us to be heard.

"I will not be teaching musical theater next year. And I'm so sorry for you. For us. For all the kids who are going to attend school here after you grow up, who won't have the same experiences that you did."

It was all for nothing. How could the district *do* this?

She scans the rows and looks into each of our disappointed faces. "Which is why from now on, musical theater will be a club, and Ms. Bishop and I will be sponsors. We'll do one play a year. This means that it will be after school, so your parents will have to provide transportation unless you live close enough to walk. Best offer. Whatcha think?"

We jump out of our chairs and yell so loud, the custodian runs in to make sure everything is okay.

"Sorry!" Ms. Harper waves, and he leaves. "Also, my condition of doing this club is that you should all greet me like that every day, forever and ever. I think that's fair."

We all laugh, and then we get to work taking apart the set.

I don't know why I do it. Maybe it's the way Aubrey's head is leaned to the side, and I recognize the same sadness in her that I see on the bus every morning. The *why* isn't important. What matters is that when I'm passing by Aubrey's seat, I say, "Hey."

She looks up at me without even moving her head. "Hey."

"I finally saw your music video. You're really talented. Maybe you'll be singing in your own video someday."

The corners of her mouth tilt up the tiniest bit. "Thanks." She fidgets with the cuff on her sleeve. "I, um, heard you were really good," she says. She looks me in the eye. "I'm sorry I missed it." She seems like she means every word.

I smile back at her. "I'm sorry you missed the play, too." What I really mean is that I'm truly sorry she didn't get to be part of it.

She nods.

And when the bell rings and I step through the double doors into the sunlight, I feel lighter.

It's a gorgeous fall day. The ground is covered with leaves, the sky is a brilliant blue, and the buses snake around the sidewalk behind the school in one continuous row. It's a good day to finally help my best friend.

I take a deep breath. It's now or never. I board the bus, and this time I don't fight it. My feet remember where I'm supposed to be.

I stop at Maddie's seat.

She looks up, her eyes wide. "Are you lost?"

That's an understatement. "I was. Can I sit?"

She stares at me like she's afraid it's another cruel joke. But then she moves over, and I drop my bag and sit down.

We wait in silence as the rest of the kids board the bus. Maddie gets out a new notebook and starts writing in it. It's okay that we're not saying anything. I'm here, where I should be.

Ben reaches the top of the steps and grins at me as he takes his seat.

*It's never too late to do the right thing.* Then why are my hands shaking?

And then Tristan and Josh slide into the seat behind us. I brace myself. This is it. This is the moment I tried so hard to avoid that it cost me my best friend.

Josh leans over the back of the seat. "Hey, look! She came back. We m-m-missed you."

I stare ahead. I can be stronger than they are. I have a voice and I will not leave.

"Did you miss us?" Josh asks.

I turn slightly so I can see what he's doing out of the corner of my eye. Tristan elbows him.

The bus pulls away from the school as Josh shakes him off. "Hey! Did I s-s-stutter?" he says with a laugh. "I asked you a question!"

My cheeks grow warm at the word "stutter," but I push through the feeling. I can't write my way out of this moment.

I have to speak up, or I might lose Maddie forever. I turn around, my voice calm as I say, "You know what? I don't c-care. If you want to make fun of me, fine. Do it if it makes you feel better. You can't hurt me anymore."

Tristan elbows him again. "Knock it off."

"What?" Josh says to Tristan.

"You heard me." Tristan's eyes meet mine, offering an apology he'll never say. "Leave her alone."

"Whatever," Josh says. "What's your problem?"

A few minutes later, Maddie puts away her notebook. "You stayed," she whispers.

"I never should've left."

She looks out the window and says nothing.

"I never should've done a lot of things." Already I feel better, and my shoulders relax slightly. If I'd just had the courage to stand by my friend in the first place, things would be so different. I wasted too much time being afraid.

She turns and considers me for a moment. "Do you have any idea what it was like?"

"No. But I hope maybe you'll t-tell me. If you want." I reach into my bag and hand her the missing red notebook.

"My notebook!" She turns it over in her hands. "I—I don't understand. What are you doing with it?"

"Someone wanted you to have it back." I shrug. "Not sure who."

She stuffs it into her bag like she's afraid it's going to disappear again. "Thanks."

"Maddie?"

"Yeah?"

"I'm sorry," I say in a quiet voice. As the words leave my mouth, an enormous weight lifts from my heart. "I never meant to hurt you." Now that I've started speaking, I can't say the words fast enough. "I made a huge mistake when I didn't sit with you, and then I was too afraid to talk to you because . . ." I take a deep breath and own exactly what I did. "I knew how wrong I was."

Maddie stares out the window at the blur of fall colors. "Well. You *are* a big chicken," she says with a hint of a smile.

I wince. "Yeah, I know. I'm working on that. I'm just so sorry, Maddie. I didn't mean any of it." The word "sorry" hangs in the air, finally out where it should be.

"I know," she says. "I read your letter."

The brakes screech as the bus approaches my stop. "I really missed you," I say as I stand up.

"Me too," she says.

Does this mean we're going to be okay? I hope so.

As soon as Lyric and I step off the bottom stair onto the pavement, I say, "Hey, I got the notebook." I don't mention her notes, even though I'm dying to tell her that I figured out her other secret, too. If she wanted me to know the notes were from her, she would tell me. But still, she had to care enough to send them. Maybe she even cares about me.

She darts a glance back at her house, like she wants to run away from me as fast as she can. "What notebook?"

"The one you slipped into my bag this morning when I wasn't looking."

"I don't know what you're talking about."

I'm not letting her wiggle out of this one. "You d-do so."

She sighs and throws up her hands. "Okay, fine. I didn't know what else to do," she says.

I know how that feels.

"I wish the thing had never landed in my lap, but when it did, I couldn't let them have it." Lyric scuffs her shoe against the curb. "I didn't speak up, and I should've. But at least I got her notebook back." She sets her jaw and glances up at me. "I had to do *something*."

I know what that's like, too. We're not so different, even though she's been pretending otherwise for a long time. I have, too.

For just a second, it's like it used to be when everything seemed so easy. Before bad choices and time changed everything, and I had a good friend just a few doors down. I miss her. A kind of hope swells in me that maybe she's still there, that she's been there the whole time. Maybe broken things can be fixed. All we need is the right words. "I gave it back to Maddie," I say.

"You didn't tell her where it came from, did you?" Lyric says, her eyes panicked. "I wouldn't want her to think that I, uh, that I had anything to do with it. I would *never.*"

"No. I won't if you won't."

"Deal," she says, relief visibly washing over her. "Thanks, Charlotte." She opens her mouth as though she's about to say something else, then closes it. She shifts her backpack and looks down at her shoes. She says, "I, um. I'm sorry. I feel so bad about last year. . . ." Her eyes meet mine, and I understand what she's trying to say. She just doesn't have the words.

I don't want this to be the end of our friendship, either. I blurt out, "You want to come over this weekend?"

A flicker of surprise crosses her face before she breaks into a smile. "Yeah. Maybe we can watch a movie or something."

"Great!" I say.

"See ya tomorrow." She starts for home.

"Hey!" I call after her.

She turns, her hair flying in the cold breeze behind her. The leaves rustle around our feet on the sidewalk.

"Why did you give the notebook to me?"

"Are you kidding? This is *you* we're talking about, Charlotte," she says with a smile. "I knew you'd do the right thing."

My eyes fill with hot tears. I wanted to do the right thing

the whole time. As I turn to go home, I plunge my hands into my jacket pockets to keep them warm. I pull a folded piece of paper out of my left pocket.

> Charlotte, I was so mad at you. Everything was bad enough, and then you did something even worse. REAL FRIENDS don't run when things get hard. But I read your letter, and it meant a lot. You can't change what you did, but you can sit with me tomorrow. I'll save you a seat.
> ♡ Maddie

I hold the note to my heart. Finally I did something right. I kick a small pebble a few feet ahead on the sidewalk, and it lands where someone has written You are extraordinary in blue chalk and dotted the *I* with a heart.

Not yet.

But I will be.

# ACKNOWLEDGMENTS

Thank you to the following people whose support means the world to me:

- Caroline Abbey, my brilliant and kind editor, who sees what could be. She is always right. It is a vulnerable thing to write a story like this one, but I knew that it—and therefore, I—would be safe with her. I could not have written this book without her tremendous heart and wisdom guiding the way.

- Jenna Lettice, for her invaluable feedback that helped shape the course of this book.

- The entire team at Random House Children's Books—I appreciate how hard they work to bring books into the world.

- Rick Richter—literary agent extraordinaire. I'm so lucky to have him on my team.

- Educators who shared their expertise—Crystal Braeuner, who walked me through the steps of school theater productions; Jennifer Sharits, who detailed speech services from the other side of the table; and Amy Beld, who affirmed more than she will ever know.

- Kari Lavelle, for her read and advice.

- Carla Bruce and Sandy Wilson, who did everything they could to help me all those years ago. I have never forgotten them.

- Susan Groenke, for telling me to write this book after she was forced to listen to the pitch in my graduation line.

- Tricia Holman Gillentine, Jo Angela Edwins, Sarah Malley, Becky Wilson, Natasha Neagle, Katie Bailey, Olivia Hinebaugh, Kesi Thomas, Danielle Selah, David Dwyer, and Matt and Leigh Ann Jernigan. They know what they did.

- My parents. They still talk to me.

- Amanda Varnes, for always being there.

Dear Reader,

I stutter. I am sometimes tempted to say I "used to stutter," as though stuttering is something in the past, from my childhood, but that isn't true or helpful to anyone. Stuttering can't be cured. After years of hard work, I still stutter sometimes, and that's okay.

It was not always okay. My speech was a source of pain for many years because of those who mocked and misunderstood it. I felt alone and different. And when, at age eleven, I needed so desperately to see myself in a book, I could not find stories about kids like me.

I did not plan to write a book about a girl who stutters. It was supposed to be about finding your voice and the bystander effect, which happens when you see someone who needs help but you don't act, because other people are there. I wanted to explore a character who was neither bully nor victim, but whose choices would inevitably determine whether she became a hero in her own story. As I worked out the details, I realized there was a missing piece. Why would someone choose not to speak, and what would it cost them? Deep down, I knew what I had to write. This was always the story that I needed to tell.

We all have had moments when we were afraid to act. For me, those moments often coincided with being too afraid to speak—at large gatherings, in class, and when a girl was tormented by bullies on my bus each day in middle school. I tried to help her, but when it backfired, I gave up. Sometimes I think back on that moment and imagine a million different scenarios. If I had been stronger. If I hadn't stuttered. If I had been popular and anyone had cared what I thought. If, if, if. It doesn't matter how I spin it. The ending remains the same.

But being a writer means I can tell a different bystander story. This one is full of big mistakes and hard choices that lead to finding your voice—not losing it. The seeds were planted long ago, when I was in middle school and I didn't know what to do.

I hope that the next time you hear someone stutter (and you eventually will), you'll think about this story. Remember how you felt when you experienced through Charlotte what it's like to stutter. Then choose to be a friend who listens and *never* mimics.

If you stutter, it does not define you. You are not alone.

And no matter who you are, even if you're afraid—*especially* if you're afraid—I hope this story sparks something that inspires you to act when you see an injustice. Do it. Write it. Use your voice to say it out loud, whatever it is.

The world is waiting for you.